To my many friends in Wales –
health, happiness, hwyl!

Contents

1

Westward Ho!

Machynlleth, Powys, Wales

'Hey, Kath . . .' Huw called through to his mother. 'Have you checked the gas bottle?'

'Yeah, it's full.'

'Did you put the Scrabble in?'

'Course I did.'

'Swimming stuff?'

'Mine's in, love. I don't know about yours.'

'Sunscreen?'

'Raincoats, more like. It's Ireland we're going to, Huw, not the Caribbean.'

'Yeah, but don't forget global warming. You need sunscreen everywhere these days.'

'Fair enough, pet. In it goes.'

'Food?'

'I've made us a packed lunch for the boat. We'll stock up on the rest when we're over there.'

'Euros?' Kath had a habit of forgetting things. Huw had a habit of reminding her.

'We've enough to be going on with,' she told him. 'We can get the rest out of a hole in the wall on the other side.'

'Road map? Remember that time we were heading for Glastonbury and ended up in Manchester . . .'

'Don't remind me, babes. I've put it in. And I've an excellent young navigator, too, thank goodness.'

'Driving licence?'

'In my wallet.'

'Passports?'

'Don't need.'

'Don't need? Are you sure?'

'Not for Ireland,' his mother insisted. 'As long as you've got ID, you're fine. Well, that's about it, I'd say,' and she clapped her hands in satisfaction. 'Can you drop the key round at Dai and Jenny's, so they pop in and feed the cats, love? I'll go and fill up the Turtle and meet you at the garage.'

'Oil, water, tyres, Kath,' Huw reminded her, as he headed out the door. 'Don't forget oil, water, tyres.'

*

'Bye, Machynlleth – see you in a week.' Huw gave a regal wave, as they drove past the leisure centre and through the only roundabout in town. Then, 'Bye, junior school – never see you again!'

'Won't you miss your friends?' his mother asked him. 'Most of them are staying on here in Mach when they move up, aren't they?'

'Everyone but me and Alice,' Huw agreed, 'but it'll be OK. I'll still see them after school. Hey, I'm really looking forward to this trip,' he said, slotting his mam's old Waterboys CD into the player. 'I've always wanted to go to Ireland.'

'Yeah, it'll be great, love,' said his mam. 'Just you, me and the Turtle heading west.'

2

Acting the Maggot

Skerries, County Dublin, Ireland

'Anyone remember to put in my golf clubs?' Mr O'Malley was doing a last-minute check before they set off on the long drive west. 'I left them next to the car.'

'I popped them in for you, dear,' said his wife, sitting next to him.

'What about my fishing gear?'

'That's in too.'

'Sure, where would I be without you, woman? So is everyone in? Have we got the lovely Leah?'

'What do you think's sitting here behind you, Da? A sack of spuds?' came the world-weary voice of a teenage girl.

'A sack of spuds is right!' laughed one of the twins, punching the other on the arm.

'OK, OK, ease up a bit, Leah, will you?' Their father was rootling about in the glove box, looking for his sunglasses. 'I mean, we're only going on holiday – it's not the end of the world, you know. Is my little Daisy-chain in?'

'Anseo,' came the voice of the youngest member of the family from behind the other three. 'I mean – here, Da.'

'Roddy and Stick? I take it that's you two, scuffling away there.'

'That's us,' sniffed the ugly one.

'Yeah, that's us, Da,' scowled the even uglier other.

'Stop kicking me, you . . .'

'I'm not, you're kicking me . . .'

'D'ya want a dig in the gob, or what?'

'Janey Mac, boys!' It was Ma this time. 'Let's go, David, before World War Three breaks out.'

'WAIT!' shrieked Daisy.

'What have you forgotten now, you silly girl?' Big-sister Leah, friendly as always. 'Your latest precious Bratz doll?'

'I'm not a silly girl – and I'd NEVER forget

my Bratz. It's Marcus!' she cried. 'We've left him behind!'

'Chance'd be a fine thing,' muttered one of the twins.

But everyone looked at everyone else. And realised Daisy was right.

*

'Marcus? Where are you, love?'

'In here. In my bedroom.'

'What on earth are you doing, son?'

'Only reading, Ma.'

'But we're going. Everyone's in the car!'

'Going?' Marcus frowned, looked up from his book. 'Oh yeah, on holiday.'

'Head in a book, as usual?' Da shook his head, as Marcus strapped himself in next to Daisy in the back row of the people-carrier.

'Brain down a drain, more like,' Leah sneered.

And nobody else said a word, not till they were well out of town.

Then, 'Wish it was me,' muttered Leah, never one to keep a grump to herself if she could inflict it on someone else.

'Wish what was you?' said Stick. 'That cow in a field over there?'

'That smiley silage bag?' Roddy was looking out of the opposite window.

'Children, children . . .' their father groaned.

'No, I wish it was me left at home, like Marcus,' said Leah.

'I'm not left at home.' Marcus looked up from his book. 'I'm here, behind you.'

'Yeah, worse luck. You nearly were, though. If it hadn't been for Daisy . . .'

'Would you just look at that beautiful bird!' cried their mother, desperate to change the subject before her youngest son realised just how close his family had come to leaving without him. And before Leah made it obvious that, but for Daisy, nobody would have even noticed that their darling brother/son was missing.

'Does anyone know what it is?' shrieked Mrs O'Malley, almost hysterically.

'Who cares, Ma?' said Roddy. 'It's just some stupid bird.'

'Actually, it's a jay,' Marcus informed them, glancing up from his book. 'You can tell by the colouring. It's all pinky-brown, with black, white and blue wings, a white bar on its lower body and a black tail . . .'

'Yeah, whatever.' Stick was unimpressed.

'Kid's a bird brain,' muttered Roddy. 'I mean, why would anyone in their right mind give a stuff about stuff like that?'

'Why would you want to be left behind, Leah?' Daisy piped up from the back. 'It's a holiday! We're off to Allihies again!'

'Ballygobackwards, you mean,' spat her teenage sister. 'Lovely for little kids, maybe . . .'

'Yeah, she'd rather be home alone with lover-boy Darren,' sneered Roddy, 'all snuggled up on the sofa, watching *Titanic* for the seven hundredth time.'

'*Titanic*'s for wusses, you wally!' hissed Leah. 'And I'm not even going out with Darren any more!'

'Oh, really?' Ma cast a glance in the mirror. 'He seemed such a nice lad.'

'That's the problem,' said Leah, under her breath. 'Too nice.'

'Yeah, keep up, Rod,' said Stick, digging his elbow into his brother's side. 'These days that no-good sister of yours'd rather be hanging out with the gangster mob. Rather be having a trash-the-house party with all her so-called mates from college.'

'You what?' muttered their father, finding it hard to concentrate on the traffic for some reason. 'A what?'

'Nothing, Da,' said Leah. 'He's only trying to wind you up, as usual.'

'Yeah, but did you hear about that wan up in town recently?' Roddy chimed in. 'Folks away. Thought she'd have a little get-together with her mates . . .'

'Word gets out . . .' said Stick.

'. . . House gets trashed,' added Roddy, with relish. 'Fifty thousand euro worth of trashed – now that's what I call a party!'

'Don't think . . .' said their da, getting the hang of the conversation at last and realising that silence was not an option, 'that your mother or I would EVER leave any one of you alone in the house while we went on holiday.'

'Better not, Da,' muttered Roddy, under his breath, 'if you want a home to come home to!'

''Cept Marcus,' said Stick. 'You'd leave him, wouldn't you, Da? Just did, in fact.'

'Yeah,' agreed Leah, 'you'd come home and find he'd read every single book in the house.'

'Too right,' said Stick. 'And put them all back on the shelves in alphabetical order. What a disaster!'

'That wouldn't be a disaster,' said Marcus, tuning in again. 'It'd be very sensible. It makes me mad the way people don't put things back where they came from, especially books. I mean, how's anyone supposed to find them the next time they need them?'

'Time somebody put you back where you came from, you wally,' muttered Roddy, under his breath. 'Six feet under, where the bookworms live!'

'Or in the vaults of Trinity Library,' said Stick. 'There's miles and miles of books, under the ground, so I heard. Let's lock him up in there.'

'And throw away the key,' added Roddy, with a grin.

'The perfect solution!' Stick rubbed his hands together. 'Hey, Da. Head into the city a minute. Clever young Marcus has just got himself a place at university . . .' he announced. 'A permanent place!'

'Would you ever stop it, boys?' said Ma. 'Couldn't you be nice to each other, for once, especially on a day like today? I mean, we're off on holiday, for goodness sake.'

'Big deal,' muttered Leah, while Roddy and Stick sawed away on imaginary fiddles.

'Just because we're stuck in a jam-jar together doesn't mean we have to be all sweety-pie,' said one.

'No way,' agreed the other.

'. . . And I don't know why you always have to pick on poor Marcus, anyway,' their mother continued.

But Marcus was used to it. And used to escaping it, too. He was deep in his book again and not even listening. It was a long way to Allihies – five hours or more, even with Da eating up the miles to try and get the dreaded journey over as quickly as possible. Might as well enjoy it, thought Marcus, turning the page.

3

Bookworms and Eejits

Allihies, County Cork, Ireland

'I'm off exploring, Kath.'

'OK, love. I'll just sort out the van.'

Huw walked down to the beach. It was beautiful. All golden red, and not a single person in sight.

They'd had a great time, crossing Ireland in the Turtle, picking out places from the *Rough Guide* to stop at. But this is what Huw'd really wanted – to get to the wild west coast, the raging Atlantic. Kath had always talked about how amazing it was – she'd been a real traveller before he was born – but this was the first time she'd ever taken Huw, and it was just as wonderful as he'd hoped.

It was only going to be the shortest of visits,

though – a taster, really – for they'd barely two days left of their holiday. Early Sunday they'd be driving to Rosslare, to get the boat back to Wales, so Huw was determined to make the most of it.

He walked the length of the beach, over to the rocks, stopping off every now and again to pick up a stone or a shell for Kath – he always tried to bring her back something interesting. Then he turned round, heading for the harbour again.

There was a boy, about his own age, up on the wall, reading a book. Huw wouldn't have minded having a chat with him, but he knew what it was like when you dived headfirst into a novel. The last thing you wanted was some stranger coming up to you – for no good reason other than that they were bored with their own company – and dragging you back into the real world.

*

That evening, after they'd eaten, Kath said she was heading up to the pub to meet the locals.

'Do you want to come in with me?' she asked.

'No thanks,' said Huw. 'I'll hang round outside. See what's happening.'

'It's OK, love. I won't embarrass you. I'll only have one pint of Guinness, and then a Ballygowan or two.'

'Whisky?'

'No, water, pet! What do you think I am?'

There were loads of kids in and around the playground, wandering up and down the street. One of them was the boy Huw had seen before, by the harbour. He was still reading.

'Good book?' said Huw, sitting down next to him on the bench.

'It's OK.'

'Who's it by?'

'Steve Voake,' said the boy.

'What, *Dreamwalker's Child*?'

'No,' said the other, turning up the cover without meeting Huw's eyes. 'The follow-up.'

'Nearly finished it, then?'

'Mmm,' said the boy, turning the page noisily.

'OK,' said Huw, who could take a hint. 'I'll leave you to it.'

*

'Are you done?' Huw had walked the length of the beach again, picked up a pocketful of shells, and was back by the harbour wall.

'Yeah.' The boy put the book down on the wall beside him.

'Any good?'

'Great! You can have it if you want.'

'That'd be brilliant,' said Huw, surprised. 'I loved the first one – got it out of the library last month. We're only here for a few days, but I'll get it back to you before we go.'

'You can keep it.'

'Huh?'

'I'm done with it. You can hang onto it.'

'Oh, right. Thanks.' Huw was amazed at such generosity, especially to a complete stranger. 'You on holiday here?'

'Yeah. You?'

Huw nodded. 'We're staying down on the site.'

'Camping?' said the other boy. 'I've always wanted to, but my da hates it. Says sleeping outdoors is for bears and hobos.'

'We're in the van, actually.'

'A VW? They're cool!'

'Ours is a beat-up old wreck. It's nice, though. We call it the Turtle.'

'Who's we?'

'Me and Kath.'

'Kath? Your big sister?'

Huw laughed. 'No, my mam, of course.'

'Your ma?'

'Yeah, what's so odd about that?'

'You call her Kath?'

'That's her name.'

'Yeah, but . . .'

'I'm Huw, by the way.'

'Oh, right . . . I'm Marcus.'

'So where are you staying, Marcus?'

'In the hostel, over the road there, next door to the pub. We come down every year.'

'You and your family?'

'Yeah. Ma and Da . . . Daisy, my little sister – that's her on the swings, I'm supposed to be keeping an eye on her . . . Roddy and Stick, my two big brothers . . . and Princess Leah.'

'Princess Leah! Like in *Star Wars*?'

'Family wars, more like. She's a pain, my big sister. Worse than toothache.'

'Massive family!' said Huw, impressed.

'Big, yeah. Hardly massive.'

'Massive compared to mine. There's only me and Kath.'

'Your ma?'

'Yeah.'

'No da?'

Huw shook his head.

'That must be weird,' said Marcus.

'Not half as weird as having five kids in the family,' said Huw, on the defensive. 'Do you have to share bedrooms, then?'

'No way. Well, I mean, yeah, we're sharing here in the hostel. Me and my brothers in one, worse luck. Leah's just with Daisy. She'd go spare if she had to bunk up with one of us.'

'How do you mean?'

'Oh, she'd scream and yell and bash the walls down. It'd be like cruelty to animals to put one of us boys in with her. You'd have to call the ISPCA.'

'RSPCA, twpsyn!'

'Huh?'

'It's RSPCA,' Huw corrected him, 'not ISPCA.'

'No, it isn't.'

'Yeah, it is – any fool knows that. The Royal Society for the Protection of Cruelty to Animals.'

'Prevention, y'eejit! And it's not Royal – it's the *Irish* Society for . . .'

'Irish? Not Royal?'

'Not Royal.'

'Ah, 'cos we're in Ireland? 'Cos there's no queen?' said Huw, understanding at last.

'Duh!' Marcus thumped his own forehead, as though it was him had been the dimwit.

'What's "y'eejit", anyway?' asked Huw.

'Huh?'

'When you said "It's not Royal, y'eejit?". What's "y'eejit"?'

'You are.'

'No, I'm not.'

'Yeah, you are.'

'OK, maybe I am,' said Huw, conceding the point. 'But what does it mean, anyway?'

'Fool. Dumbo. Amadan. Eejit.'

Huw got it – from the first two words, at least. 'Ah!' he said. 'As in i-di-ot.' He pronounced it clearly, stressing all three syllables.

'Suppose so. Never thought of it.'

'So who's the eejit now then, y'eejit?' Huw laughed. 'Oh, I'm from Wales, by the way, in case you hadn't realised.'

'That explains it! I thought you were from the planet Mars for a minute there. I've never been to Wales,' said Marcus, with a shrug. 'Is it nice?'

'Nice? It's God's Own Country!'

'No way! That's Ireland.'

'No, it's not.'

'Sure, it is.'

'So it's three rooms, is it?' said Huw, trying to get the conversation back on track.

'Huh?'

'Three rooms in the hostel. Must cost you a fortune.'

'Sure, hostels are only cheap. We usually stay in proper hotels, when we're away. It's just that my da and ma met here, when they were young, so they've a soft spot for the place.' Marcus shrugged again. 'We come down for the last week in August every year. Have been forever.'

'Hotels! Your folks must be rich. Me and Kath never pay to stay anywhere, except on campsites. So you've all got your own rooms at home then, have you?'

'Course we have. You don't think I'd sleep with Roddy and Stick, do you? They're a complete pain, those two.'

'Yeah, but that means your house has, what, six bedrooms? That's enormous.'

'Yeah, well, I suppose it's big enough . . .'

'Big enough for an army! Have you a garden, as well?'

'Course we have. There's a pool round the back, too, sort of. Oh, and a bit of a tennis court down in the orchard.'

'A tennis court! You must be millionaires!'

'Nah. Well, I suppose Da's pretty loaded, if you count the house . . . and the business . . . and the cars and stuff.'

'What does he do, then?' Huw was intrigued. He didn't know any rich people. Not seriously rich. 'It'd take my mam about five hundred years to earn that much money. She only works part-time, in a plant nursery.'

'Builder. Not that he gets his hands dirty these days, but you know what I mean. Ma works in a bank.'

'Wow!' Huw blinked, like he'd been looking at the sun too long.

'Wow, what?'

'Just wow. Five kids, six bedrooms, a tennis court in the orchard, and a million quid in the bank, owned by your mam . . .'

'She doesn't exactly own the bank. And it's euro, not pounds, y'eejit.'

'Same difference. And stop calling me y'eejit,' said Huw. 'Me and Kath, all we've got is two cats, two bedrooms, no garden and a tiny terraced house next to the Co-op in downtown Machynlleth.'

'Downtown where?'

'Machynlleth.'

'What's that when it's at home?'

'It's home.'

'Oh, right. Welsh, is it?'

'Course it's Welsh. It's in Wales, stupid.'

'They speak funny there, don't they?' said Marcus.

'How do you mean?'

'Funny accents. All uchs and huchs.'

'No more funny than here,' said Huw, defensively.

'Well it sounds funny to me.'

'That's 'cos you're Irish.'

'Yeah, maybe. Anyway, just 'cos we've a big house doesn't mean we've got everything,' said Marcus. 'I mean, you've got a camper van and we haven't . . .'

'Yeah. Me and Kath – we're Turtelaires!' Huw smiled, ironically. 'We're rich!'

4

The Perfect Spit

Allihies, County Cork, Ireland

'Oh, hi, Daisy,' said Marcus, as his little sister came past. 'You ready to go back to the hostel?'

'Wow!' Daisy was pointing at Huw.

'It's rude to point,' Marcus told her. 'Huw, this is Daisy,' he said, introducing them to one another. 'Daisy . . . Huw . . .'

'Double wow!' said his sister, looking from one to another.

'Cut the wowing, Daisy,' Marcus told her. 'And cut the gawking, too.'

'What's up?' Huw asked her. 'You look like you've seen a ghost or something.'

'You're the spit!' Daisy's eyes were nearly popping out of her head.

'What do you mean?'

'You . . .' she said, pointing again, 'and Marcus . . .'
She turned to her brother. 'You're the absolute spit of
one another!'

'The spit?' Huw decided to tease her. 'As in . . .'
And he hoiked up a gobbet and splattered it at her
feet.

'Eek!' Daisy jumped back, checked Huw's face to
see if he was smiling, and then smiled in return.

'No, y'eejit,' Marcus was laughing at his new-
found friend. 'Don't they even speak English in
Wales at all? She thinks we look alike.'

'More than alike!' cried Daisy. 'You're peas in a pod!'

Huw looked at the other boy, to see what his little
sister was on about. 'Same colour hair, I suppose,' he
said, with a shrug. 'That's about it, really, isn't it?
What do you think, Marcus?'

Marcus looked back at him, frowning. 'Same sort
of height, maybe.'

'Oh, Marcus!' Daisy stamped her foot in
frustration. 'You're the spit! It's obvious!'

But the other two just shrugged their shoulders,
and looked at her as though she was mad. And
there's nothing more likely to make you mad than

people looking at you as though you're mad –
especially if one of them's your big brother.

'Come here with me, then, the both of you,' said
Daisy, determined to prove she was right. 'We'll ask
someone who doesn't know you . . .'

And she led them to a girl about their own age,
over on the swings.

'This is Sorks,' she told them. 'She's my little-
while friend, aren't you, Sorks?'

'Yeh,' said the girl, swinging her long legs high.

Marcus looked – and looked away. Girls his own
age were embarrassing enough. Girls with long bare
legs, way up above you, were too much altogether.

'Which one of these do you think's my brother,
Sorks?' Daisy asked her.

The girl looked from one to the other as she
swung downwards, and a broad grin spread across
her face. 'Twinnies!' she shrieked. 'I love twinnies!'

'We're not twins!' Marcus was horrified. 'We've
never even met before tonight.'

'Yeh, right . . .' said the girl, dragging her feet on
the ground and coming to an abrupt halt. 'There's
no way ye can hide it, not when ye're identi-tickle,
like ye lads. No need to do a reddener, though,' she

said, seeing Marcus's face turn to the colour of his hair. He never normally talked to girls much. Not ones his own age, anyway. And especially not ones as pretty as Sorks.

'Ye're twins, and that's the pure truth of it,' she said, looking from Huw to Marcus and back again. 'Ye're not related to Daisy, though. Ye're way too ugly.'

'Gee, thanks,' said Huw, amused. 'What sort of a name's Sorks, anyway? Sounds like a cross between a stork and a pair of socks.'

'Ye think ye're funny, don't ye? said the girl. 'It's Sorcha, if ye must know.'

'That's even odder. How do you spell it?'

'S-O-R-C-H-A.'

'Oh, Sorch-a,' said Huw, pronouncing it like torch-a. 'I've seen it written down. I didn't know it was Irish.'

'Don't know much then, do ye?' said the girl. 'So what's your name, so?'

'Huw.'

'As in Huge?' said Sorks, grinning.

'No, as in Huw, as a matter of fact. H-U-W.'

'Huh?'

'No, not huh – Huw.'

'Ah, Hugh!'

'That's what I said, twpsyn.'

Sorcha frowned. 'Yeh, but ye don't spell it H-U-W . . .'

'You think I don't know how to spell my own name?'

'Well, ye seem to think I don't know how to pronounce mine!'

'So how would YOU spell it, then?' Huw asked her.

'H-U-G-H,' said Sorks. 'That's how ye write Hugh, isn't it, twinnie-boy?' she said, looking at Marcus.

'Yeah. Or A-O-D-H,' muttered Marcus, looking at his feet. 'And I'm not a twinnie.'

'A-O-D-H?' said Huw. 'What's that when it's at home?'

'Aodh,' said Marcus. 'It's the Irish for Hugh.'

'Ay!' said Huw, pronouncing it the way Marcus had. 'That's weird! It's like a name with just one letter.'

'Nothing weird about that,' said Daisy. 'I've got an aunty called Kay – that's only one letter, too.'

'No, it's not, it's three,' said Huw.

'One,' repeated Daisy.

'Three,' insisted Huw.

'And there's an Aunty Em in *The Wizard of Oz*,' added Marcus, deciding to back his sister up.

'That's got two letters,' said Huw. 'I've read the book.'

'Oz or Em?'

'Em,' said Huw.

'You're wrong. It's only got one,' said Daisy, shaking her head at him. 'I've seen the film.'

'And there's a couple of friends of mine at school . . .' said Sorcha, deciding to keep it going. 'One's called Bee and the other's Dee, so there!'

'They don't count,' said Huw. 'They're only nicknames. They're probably really Branwen and Delyth or something . . .'

'Branwen and Delyth!' Sorcha laughed. 'What sort of names are they?'

'Good Welsh names,' Huw told her.

'They're hardly likely to have Welsh names, living round here, now are they?' Sorcha raised her eyes to heaven. 'But you're wrong, Mr Know-It-All. Bee and Dee really are their proper names. I've seen their birth certificates.'

'See!' said Daisy. 'Bee, Dee, Em and Kay . . . There's loads of names with just one letter – that's four already.'

'She's right,' agreed Sorcha. 'So what's wrong with Aodh?' she said, turning to Huw. 'It's just as good a name as Branwen or Delyth, anyway!'

'It's weird, that's all,' said Huw. 'It's just a weird way to spell it.'

'No more weird than H-U-W!'

'Way more weird!' Huw was determined to keep fighting his corner, even though the whole of Ireland seemed to be lined up against him. 'And A-O-D-H doesn't even look like A, never mind sound like Huw!'

'That's 'cos it's Irish, ye dimwit,' said Sorks. 'Ye can't expect a word in one language to look and sound like a word in another.'

'Exactly,' said Huw. 'Which is why Huw doesn't look the same as Hugh, tho' in this case they're the same name, and they sound the same too, which is a lot handier than . . .'

'Huh?' Sorcha was lost.

'Not, huh, Huw! How many times do I have to tell you, girl?' said Huw. 'It's Welsh!'

'Ah.' Understanding dawned across her face. 'You're Welsh, like!'

'You make it sound like I'm from outer space or something!'

'Well, not exactly outer space,' said Sorcha. 'But ye're definitely an alien, round here.'

Huw laughed. 'So are you from round here, then?'

'Yeh,' said the girl. 'County Cork, born and bred. We were living in Bantry till last year – that's over the road a bit . . .'

'Yeah, we came through on the way, I think,' said Huw.

'Hey, I just love your accent! Ye speak kind of up-and-down, like.' Sorcha beamed, delighted. 'Wow, twinnies and Welshies in one day! Massive!'

'I told you – we're NOT twinnies.' Huw shook his head. 'And what about your accent, anyway? It's up-and-down like I've never heard before.' He raised his voice high, 'Say it loud and say it clear, I'm the Welsh boy, over here!'

'Say it clear, say it loud – say you're Irish, say it proud!' countered Marcus. 'Sure, we'll beat you hollow at the rugby – next time, anyway.'

'No chance,' said Huw, with a laugh. 'The dragon's on fire again, and it'll take more than a bunch of Paddies to put it out.'

'You're funny, Huw,' said Daisy. 'You talk funny. And you look funny, too.'

'Gee, thanks,' said Huw.

'Yeah, thanks, sister,' said Marcus. 'That means I look funny too, if we're identi-tickle, like you say.'

And everyone laughed, as Daisy ran across the playground. 'Look in here,' she called, from over by the slide. She was pointing down at the shiny metal.

They wandered over behind her and looked. 'I can see two boys,' said Huw, wondering what she was up to.

'With curly red hair,' added Marcus, standing beside him and staring down.

'See, I told you,' said Daisy. 'And four sticky-out ears!'

'Two pointy noses and a rake of freckles between ye,' said Sorks, striding up behind them and laughing. 'Daisy's right. Ye're the perfect spit, ye two.'

Marcus glared at her. Huw did, too.

'And daggers in your deep blue eyes,' said Sorks, delightedly. 'Ye've both got them!'

5

Cork-ovision

Allihies, County Cork, Ireland

'Hey, Marcus! Daisy! Da says it's time you were back at the hostel!' It was Leah, arm-in-arm with a local lad.

'Doesn't take her long . . .' muttered Marcus.

'Let's see if there's a Friday night sing-song,' suggested Sorks.

'How do you mean?' asked Huw.

'Over in the hostel. Sometimes Seamus, who runs the place, lights a fire in the courtyard and gets his guitar out.'

So Huw popped his head round the door of the pub. Kath was up at the bar, chatting away.

'All right, babes?' she said, when she spotted him. 'Want a coke?'

All eyes turned towards Huw. He wanted to shrink into the ground. It was bad enough having the whole pub staring at him, but eleven years old, and still being called 'babes' and 'pet'! He was going to have to have a word with Kath, once and for all.

'I'm OK,' he muttered. 'I'll just be next door at the hostel. There's a sing-song in the yard.'

'I'll be there now, in a minute. Just finish my Ballygowan.'

> *'Whack fol de Daddy-oh,*
> *There's whisky in the jar!'*

There were loads of people, young and old, local and not-so-local, hanging around the yard. Most of them were joining in the chorus.

'Is that the lovely Sorks I see?' It was Seamus, the hostel owner, up at the front, with his guitar. 'Will you give us a song, girl?' he said, beckoning her forward.

'Ah no, not tonight,' muttered Sorcha.

But Seamus was having none of it. 'Sure, hasn't this handsome young lady the finest voice this side of the Eurovision Song Contest? Let's hear it for Miss Sorcha McNulty, the Bantry canary . . .'

'Sorcha! Sorcha!' went the crowd, and Sorks, knowing there'd be no escape, and not really minding anyway, stepped forward into the firelight and held up her hand for a bit of hush.

Everything went still, but for the cracking of sticks in the fire.

> *'Tá mé mo shuí,*
> *O d'éirigh an ghealach aréir . . .'*

She sang a beautiful sad song in Irish, all six verses of it, and everyone listened, right to the end. It was like the whole night stilled as she sang, and there was a silence, long after she'd finished, as everyone let the power of the music sink deep into their bones.

Huw found himself the first to clap, and then wished he hadn't.

'Come on then, Huge,' whispered Sorcha, who'd melted back into the crowd and was squeezing onto the log next to him. 'Everyone says the Welsh are the best singers in the world, especially the men.'

'Ah no,' said Huw. 'I wouldn't know what to sing.'

'Sure, everyone has a song in them. What's that one ye do in the rugby?'

Huw frowned.

'Or are ye too embarrassed?' she said, grinning.

So Huw, who never normally sang in public, not on his own anyway, felt he'd no option. He got to his feet, turned to face the crowd, opened his mouth, and soon found his heart filling with pride.

> *'Calon lân yn llawn daioni*
> *Tecach yw na'r lili dlos . . .'*

Everyone listened in silence, even the kids in the corner. And when he was finished, they all clapped and cheered and joked about the rugby.

Then Kath arrived, amid the hubbub of appreciation. She peered into the darkness of the courtyard, surprised to see so many people. Wandering round, she tried to pick out her son among all the strangers. Which wasn't easy, considering how the only light was from the flickering of the campfire, and most of the older children seemed to be huddling in the darkest corners.

'Come on, Huw,' she said at last, spotting him by the wall. 'It's time we were getting back, babes.'

Only what she didn't realise was that she hadn't said it to Huw, she'd said it to Marcus.

*

'Who's that woman?' Marcus hissed, out of breath.

'What, that one over by there? That's Kath – my mam.'

'She just called me Huw!' said Marcus, horrified.

'She didn't!'

'She did. She called me "babes" too!'

'That's her, all right,' said Huw, tutting. 'But Daisy must be right. If even Kath can't tell the difference between us, we really must be the spit!'

'. . . and that girlfriend of yours,' said Marcus, slightly enviously. 'She must be right, too.'

'What girlfriend?'

'Sorks.'

'Don't be an eejit!' said Huw, latching onto his newest favouritest word.

'She's not my girlfriend. I only just met her.'

'She didn't really call you Huw, though – my mam, I mean?'

'She did, I swear,' said Marcus, nodding. 'She's nice, though, by the look of her.'

'Who, Sorks? I knew it was you who fancied her!'

'No way,' said Marcus. Luckily it was too dark to see him blushing. 'No, I mean your ma! Wish I had me ma just to myself, sometimes. She's always so busy, what with the job and the big house and Daisy and . . .'

'Well, to tell you the truth, sometimes I wish I'd a big family, like you have,' said Huw. 'I can see Daisy could be annoying sometimes, but she's a good laugh.'

'Yeah, maybe, but Roddy and Stick!' said Marcus. 'And the dreaded Princess Leah? I wouldn't wish them on my worst enemy.'

'I'm not saying anything against Kath.' Huw was worried all of a sudden that he'd been disloyal to his mother. 'I mean, me and her, we get on really well. She never bosses me about or nothing . . .'

'Lucky you! I get bossed about by everyone, all the time,' said Marcus. 'Da does it, and Ma, too. Leah does it every time she sees me. Roddy and Stick are always at it. Even Daisy'd boss me around, if I let her.'

'Yeah, but maybe the trouble with being your mam's best friend . . .' It was the first time Huw had put into words how he felt about being a single child of a single mother, and the train of thought was taking him over, somehow – '. . . is that you can't just go off and do your own thing any time you want. Sometimes, if I feel like reading a book or hanging out with my mates, it's like I should be spending time with her, instead. Keeping her company, or something . . .'

'She's lonely? Is that what you mean?'

'Yeah, I suppose she is. And it ends up making me a bit lonely too, 'cos I'm sort of stuck at home with her . . .'

'You don't seem lonely. You're much more, eh, open than me. You must have loads of friends. And girlfriends.'

'Friends, yeah. And friends that are girls, some of them. But girlfriends? Nah, I don't really do girlfriends,' said Huw, shaking his head. 'Not in the way you mean, anyway. Maybe it comes from it being just me and Kath. I'm OK at talking to them, but anything more – it'd be like letting Mam down, somehow . . .'

'What, like betraying her?'

'Sort of . . .'

'You're brill at talking to them, though – girls, that is. Way better than me, anyway. Did you see me with Sorks?'

'Yeah, well, you're just shy with them, that's all. But she fancied you, I can tell.'

'She did not!'

'Did.'

'It was you she fancied, not me!' said Marcus. 'It's you she was talking to, wasn't it?'

'Yeah, but only 'cos you're so quiet. She said we looked the same, so if she fancies me, she must fancy you, too. Tell you what, go up and sit next to her and see what she does – I dare you.'

'No way. Why?'

'Just to see.'

'See what?'

'See what happens. See if she talks to you.'

'Nah. I couldn't. Not on my own.'

'Course you could.'

'What if she just ignores me?'

'Then do the talking yourself. She won't though.'

'You sure?'

'Yeah. Go on. She won't bite your head off. Or do you want to be a wuss all your life?'

*

Sorcha was sitting on a log, with the firelight dancing on her face.

'Is anyone . . .?' Marcus's voice trailed off and he felt like disappearing.

But Sorcha glanced up, smiled and edged over to make room. Marcus lowered himself down and perched on the log, trying as hard as he could not to make physical contact. It wasn't really possible, though. As bits of them actually touched, Marcus blushed to the roots.

Sorcha didn't seem the slightest bit bothered. He could tell she was lost in the music, and in the magic of the warm summer's night.

They sat there side by side, one swaying, the other completely still. Marcus was waiting for her to say something. But she didn't.

He tried to think of something to say. But he couldn't.

He thought he'd feel uncomfortable. But he didn't.

Next thing, though, he was shocked to feel Sorcha leaning her head into his shoulder. He felt the warmth of her.

Then something even more amazing happened as Sorcha's fingers, dreamily dancing to the jig of the music, somehow managed to dance their way into his, tangle themselves tight, and stay there. Marcus could hardly believe it. He was holding hands with a girl!

He held his breath, unable to speak, and then the most astonishing thing of all . . . Sorcha, eyes closed, slowly turned her face to his, reached up and kissed him!

'Mmmm . . .' she murmured, with the warmest of smiles in her voice, '. . . Huge!'

Marcus leapt to his feet and ran.

6

Peas in a Pod

Allihies, County Cork, Ireland

'I've got a plan,' gasped Marcus, when he'd found Huw again. He'd no intention of mentioning the kiss, though – it was way too embarrassing. Especially knowing it only happened, he was sure, because Sorks had mistaken him for Huw.

'Tell me.' Huw was interested. He liked plans.

'Well, you know how we were talking about families and stuff . . .'

'Yeah.'

'Well, you know how I was saying about how I'm fed up with being, sort of, invisible . . .' said Marcus.

'Invisible?'

'Yeah, like my lot are all so caught up in their

own busy lives that I don't think they really care what I'm up to, most of the time. In fact, sometimes I don't think they'd even notice if I dropped off the face of the planet.'

'Mmm?'

'And you know you were saying how you quite fancied being a part of a bigger family for once.'

'I think I know where you're coming from here,' said Huw, slowly. 'Like a family with loads of dosh, you mean?'

'Yeah.'

'And a swimming pool in the garden?'

'Absolutely.'

'Not to mention a tennis court?'

'That's the one.'

'With a son who gets loads of pocket money every week?'

'Buckets of the stuff!' Marcus was happy to exaggerate at this point, so he didn't feel the need to mention that the pool was more of a pond, really – fine for frogs, but not exactly Olympic standard.

And that the tennis court wasn't actually a tennis court as such, more like a tennis-court-shaped piece of hard-standing where his dad stored his dead JCBs and stuff. More Wimpey than Wimbledon, but you can always dream, can't you?

'And lives by the sea . . .?' Huw carried on. 'In Ireland.'

'He sure does.' Marcus had a feeling he was onto a winner by this time. 'So you know how everyone seems to think we look so much alike?'

'Peas in a pod,' said Huw.

'The perfect spit,' said Marcus.

'Yeah.' Huw laughed. 'I'm the perfect one. You're the spit.'

'Other way round, fella,' said Marcus. And he hoicked up a gobbet of spit, and landed it just outside Huw's right leg.

'Oi!' cried Huw. 'That nearly landed on my trousers!' He placed his foot on the splat and returned fire, just missing Marcus's right leg.

'Splitsies!' said Marcus, firing one back.

'No – spitsies!' cried Huw, in return, and the game carried on, each having to stretch their legs wider and wider to reach the spits. Careful, too, not to slip on the grass which was getting more and more slimy and disgusting.

'So anyway,' said Marcus, when he couldn't

stretch his legs an inch wider without doing himself a damage. 'If we're really so much alike, as everyone seems to think. And if we both fancy a bit of a change of lifestyle . . .'

'Why don't we SWAP!' cried Huw, getting in before his newfound friend.

But Marcus put his finger to his lips. 'Shush!' he said, throwing a glance all around, to check no one had heard. 'It's got to be our little secret.'

'It's a great idea,' said Huw, trying to contain his giggles. 'But it's ridiculous. I mean, we can't possibly do it.'

'I don't see why not,' said Marcus. 'Just for a laugh. See how long it takes them to notice.'

'Is this about you and Sorks?' asked Huw, frowning. 'Do you want to pretend to be me, so she'll . . .'

'No fear! I'm staying well clear of her. I just think it'd be fun, that's all. And sort of interesting, too. See what it's like being someone else. How it feels in someone else's shoes.'

'And clothes,' said Huw. 'We'd have to swap clothes, too. It's the only way they can tell us apart, as it is.'

'Yeah, I can just see you in me jammers! Oh, and accents . . .' said Marcus. 'You'll have to speak Irish and I'll have to speak Welsh.'

'I don't think we can do that.' Huw shook his head. 'I mean, do you know any Welsh? I certainly don't know any Irish.'

'I don't mean the language, silly. Just the accent.'

'I'm still not too sure. I'll sound like Father Ted.'

'Yeah, and I'll sound like that guy, you know, the only gay in wherever-it-is . . .'

They both burst into fits of giggles.

'I think, if we do it, we'd better just keep hush, don't you think?'

'Yeah. It'll be night, anyway.' Marcus agreed. 'All we gotta do is snore.'

'In Welsh,' said Huw. 'Like a sheep on Snowdon.'

'Or in Irish,' countered Marcus. 'Like a pig in peat.'

Huw gave him a look. 'And then, in the morning . . .' he began. 'Ah, we'll worry about that when the morning comes. We'll just play along with it and see how long it takes for anyone to find out.'

'I bet your ma's the first to work out what we're up to,' said Marcus. 'You two talk to each other all the time. And you're sharing the van, so there's no escape. She'll realise I'm not her true-born son before I've even had my breakfast.'

'Not if you keep your mouth shut,' Huw told him. 'Pretend you've got a headache or something. She's not much of a morning person, anyway – never says or sees much before she's had a couple of mugs of strong coffee, especially after a late night.'

'Yeah, and what you've got to do is just grunt when Roddy and Stick wake up,' Marcus advised him. 'It's all those two do anyway – grunt and fart.'

'Oh, lovely,' said Huw, with a laugh. 'I can't wait.'

'So are you up for it?' Marcus asked him. 'Just for tonight, like.'

'Why not?' Huw'd been won over by the other boy's enthusiasm. 'Me, here in the hostel, and you, head off back to the Turtle? See how long it takes Kath to work out it's not me?'

'Yeah, you can borrow a clothes-peg for your nose . . .' Marcus rummaged about in his pocket. 'No, sorry – I can't find one. You'll just have to make sure the window's wide open. You don't want to be suffocated by the smell of feet and f . . .'

'Come on, show me where you're sleeping,' said

Huw. 'Then I'll take you down to the Turtle. 50p says I'm the winner.'

'50c you mean.'

'Huh?' Huw frowned. 'You mean ceiniog?'

It was Marcus's turn to frown.

'Ceiniog,' repeated Huw. 'It's Welsh for pence.'

'Don't be an eejit – it's cents, not pence,' exclaimed Marcus. 'You're in Europe now, not some great British empire!'

'Oh yeah, euros, sorry,' said Huw. 'OK, you give me 50p worth, my money, if I last longer than you. I'll give you 50 cents yours, if you're the one who wins.'

'I'm up for a bet,' said Marcus. 'But 50 cents is nothing. And neither's 50 pence. Let's make it fifty an hour.'

'Fifty an hour?' Huw was alarmed.

'Yeah,' said Marcus. 'If I survive four hours without being recognized, then you owe me two euro.'

'And if I survive four hours,' said Huw, thinking about it, 'you owe me two quid.'

'If I last the night, you owe me, oh, about four euro,' Marcus calculated.

'Four euro!' Huw was worried now. 'That's loads!'

'Don't be daft,' said Marcus. 'Sure, I get ten a week.'

'Ten euro a week – that's about seven quid!' Huw was amazed. Nobody he knew got anywhere near that.

Marcus frowned at him. 'Why, how much pocket money do you get?'

'One.'

'One pound?' Marcus couldn't believe his ears. 'Your ma must be right stingy.'

'No, she's not,' said Huw, crossly. 'We just haven't got as much money as you. Not everybody in the world's a millionaire, you know.'

'Yeah, but one pound!' said Marcus. 'You can hardly buy a Yorkie bar with that.'

And it might have developed into a real argument, only both of them realised and backed down.

'That's why I do a paper round before school,' Huw told him. 'To make a bit of extra money. Comes in handy, it does. Except I won't be able to any more, now I've got to catch the early bus to Aber.'

And then his thoughts returned to the deal that Marcus was offering. And how he couldn't lose, not really, because with pence worth way more than cents, he stood to make a tidy profit, even if they both lasted the same amount of time.

'OK,' he said. 'Your fifty an hour against my fifty.' He spat into the palm of his hands, rubbed them together, and offered one to Marcus to shake.

Marcus looked at it and frowned. But then he took his courage in both hands, spat into his own, rubbed them together and shook.

'The perfect spit?' said Huw, as slime met slime.

'The perfect spit!' said Marcus, grimacing.

They wiped their slimy palms on their trousers, and forced a smile.

7

The Swap

Allihies, County Cork, Ireland

'This bed's mine,' Marcus whispered to Huw, pointing to the one by the wall. 'Just climb in, and if you hear anyone coming into the room, pretend you're asleep.'

'Closest to the window?' said Huw. 'Makes sense.' And he went over and opened it wide. 'Where's the dreaded Roddy and Stick, anyway?'

'Oh, out and about. They hang out with the locals. Don't come back till late.'

'So when your dad called you back in . . .'

'That was only me and Daisy. The other three can do what they like, pretty much. You'll hear them when they do come in, though. Blasting the lights on. Stomping about like a herd of elephants. Effin' and blindin' and getting shushed by all the people in the other rooms.'

'I can't wait,' said Huw, raising his eyebrows. 'Right, let's get changed.'

'Here and now?'

'Yeah, here and now.'

So, trying to suppress their giggles, they both stripped off down to their pants and put on each other's clothes.

'I can sort of see what Daisy means,' said Marcus, looking in the mirror.

'Yeah. Me, too,' said Huw. 'Hey, close your eyes for five seconds . . .' And he stepped away, on tippy-toes. 'Now open them and tell me who you're looking at.'

Marcus shut his eyes tight, opened them wide, then scratched his chin. 'Duh . . . I dunno!'

And they both laughed, over and over until there was no stopping them – or not until they fell onto the beds and rolled off onto the floor, clutching their bellies.

'Shhhh,' said Huw, when he'd managed to pull himself together. 'Next step, the Turtle. With any luck, Kath'll be sleeping it off by now, and won't hear a thing.'

*

Which is exactly what happened.

Huw led his double to the site, double-quick (luckily he had a torch with him, so they didn't go tripping over guy ropes and tent pegs, like you do when you're wandering round a campsite at night – especially when you're chock-full of giggles). He had a peek round the door of the van and, when he saw Kath fast asleep in her bed, pushed it shut again, and proceeded to give Marcus a long list of whispered instructions as to where things were and what the morning routine was.

'And don't call her "y'eejit",' he whispered. 'You're supposed to be Welsh, remember.'

'Sure, why would I want to go and do that?' replied Marcus, laying on the accent. 'D'you think I'm a right eejit, or what?'

'Pob lwc, bach,' said Huw, turning to go.

Marcus frowned.

'It means good luck, mate,' Huw told him. 'I'll see you in the morning.'

'Or earlier,' said Marcus. 'Hey, Huw – if your ma wakes up and discovers I'm an impostor, will she be mad at me?'

'A bit surprised, maybe. But she's got a good sense of humour. I think she'll see the funny side.'

*

Huw headed back to the hostel.

'How's the craic, kid?' said a voice as he entered the room. Oh no, the boys were back before him.

Huw looked round the walls. What crack? Where?

'So where've you been till now, little bruv?' said another voice. 'How come you're in so late?'

'Oh, just out and about,' replied Huw, using the phrase Marcus had used earlier. Only he couldn't quite manage to say it in his best Irish accent without blushing.

'Hey, look at the beamer on that fella!' said Roddy to Stick, or Stick to Roddy (Huw hadn't a clue which was which). 'I'd say he's pulled! Have you pulled a bird, kid? Bout time, too!'

'No way!' Huw blushed to the roots of his redness.

'Marky's got a girlfriend! Marky's got a girlfriend! Come on, what's the story, Jackanory?' said the terrible twins, piling in on him. 'Spill the beans . . .'

'Sod off!' Huw pushed them away, grabbed Marcus's pyjamas from under the pillow and ran to the bathroom.

'Cooled the jets yet, kid?' said one of the brothers when he got back.

'Yeah, what's rattled your cage?' said the other. 'Didn't she fancy a ginger minger?'

But Huw just stuck out his tongue and refused to answer, in the hope that they'd get the message and leave him alone. And it worked, amazingly, for the other two were so surprised at their meek and mild little brother going all uppity with them that they actually shut up.

'Let him stew,' said one, and they settled down for a quiet night's sleep. Apart from the snoring and the farting, of course – Marcus had been right about that. Within twenty minutes the room smelled, and sounded, like the lion enclosure at Chester Zoo. Ych a fi!

8

Trouble Looms

Allihies, County Cork, Ireland

Doodly-dip-doodly-doo-doodly-diddly-diddly-doo . . .

'Where is it? Oh for goodness sake.' Kath fumbled for her mobile, trying to kill the stupid tune before it woke Huw.

'Hello,' she whispered. 'Who . . .?'

'Hello, Kath? Milly Baker, here. I'm a friend of your mother's.'

'Who? What? How did you get my number? It's the middle of the night.' And then Kath twigged. 'Is something wrong? Has something happened to Mum?'

'She's not in any danger, Kath,' said the voice at

the other end. 'But she's had a bad fall. She's in hospital. She's broken her arm.'

'What? How? I bet it was that damn bike. I keep telling her she's too . . .'

'Kath. Listen to me. Yes, it was a fall from her bike, on the way home from Bingo. But it's not just her arm . . .'

'What do you mean? What is it?'

'She hit her head on the edge of the pavement. They're keeping her in hospital, to monitor her progress. They think . . .' The voice at the other end went quiet.

'Think what?' Kath managed to keep to a whisper, despite the news. She didn't want to wake her son. Not before she at least knew the full story. 'Tell me!' she hissed.

'They've done some X-rays. They're waiting for a second opinion, but they think it's just possible she's fractured her skull.'

'Fractured her skull!'

'Just a hairline fracture, if anything, they said, but . . .'

'I bought her SIX different helmets!' Kath was frantic now – still speaking quietly, but very, very upset. 'One to match each of her outfits, but could I get her to wear one? "What's the point in paying to have your hair done twice a week if you're going to go and squash it into a helmet?" she'd say. Oh, Milly – which hospital's she in?'

'Chester General. But it sounds like they might have to transfer her to the John Lennon in Liverpool. They've a special Head Injury Unit there. She'll be in excellent hands.'

'Oh, why wasn't I there?' moaned Kath. 'Why didn't I get her to come and live with us?' Then, 'Right,' she said, trying to pull herself together. 'I'll ring the hospital now and see what they say.'

'Good idea, love. They won't tell me much because I'm not family – you'll probably get a whole lot more out of them than I could. How long do you think it'll be before you can get here?'

'I'm over in Ireland on holiday, but I'll head back straight away. I can be there in the morning – Chester or Liverpool, wherever she is.'

'That's great. I'm sure your mum'll be really pleased to see you.'

'Thanks, Milly, for letting me know what's

happened. It was really good of you. How did you track me down, anyway?'

'I'd been at the Bingo with her. Came out just as she was cycling off, and saw it happen. I was right shocked, I can tell you. But once I'd called the ambulance and made her as comfortable as I could, I had a rootle through her stuff – I knew I had to let someone in her family know. I found her mobile in her bag and looked through the numbers for anyone called Kath – she's always talking about you and that grandson of hers.'

'Thank you so much, Milly. You're a real life-saver.'

*

'Right . . .' Kath was always one for muttering to herself. It's what comes of living alone. Well, sort of alone. 'Put the bed away. Disconnect the gas. Wake Huw? No, let him sleep. Poor kid, it's going to be such a horrible end to the holiday. And he was having such a good time, too. Oh well, we can always come back, I suppose.

'Poor Mum, though. My poor, poor mum. I'll be

all right, driving, anyway. Thank goodness I only had the one pint of Guinness. Quite like night driving, really – no traffic – just me and the road. When's the first boat, I wonder? Now what did I do with that brochure? Ah, here it is. Ten-thirty, Rosslare. Hmm, bit late, that. Why don't I go back on the Dublin to Holyhead, instead? Wouldn't take me much longer, and it'd be much more convenient for driving on to Chester or Liverpool. Yeah, good idea, Kath – I'm sure they'd transfer my ticket, especially if I explain. Dublin to Holyhead, let's see . . . Ah, eight o'clock on the Fast Ferry, and a hundred minutes to Wales. Perfect. Six hours' driving time, if I get a move on. Get there for around seven. I'd better hit the road.

'Poor Mum, lying there with your head all broken. Never would learn to drive, would you? Green before your time. But why, oh why, did you always insist on riding that ancient old rattletrap bike everywhere, even at night? No helmet. Rubbishy brakes, too, probably. Bet the lights weren't even working. Oh, Mum – I love you so much, but you're as stubborn as a mule. Why oh why will you never listen?'

In the back of the van, Marcus, who'd had to

develop the skills of sleeping deeply, especially on holiday with Roddy and Stick, was lost to the world – completely one hundred per cent unaware that the engine had started up. That the rattly old van was edging its way out of the campsite and heading off up the Beara peninsula, along the empty road hugging the coastline up to Kenmare, then picking up speed on the long journey east, over the darkened roads of Ireland and all the way to Dublin. Unaware that, unless he was to wake up soon, he'd be well on the way to Wales.

9

Feet and Farts

Allihies, County Cork, Ireland

Huw slept. Or tried to. But, ych a fi, what was it about these two, he thought? Did they EVER change their socks? I mean, they're supposed to be millionaires, sort of, aren't they? OK, million-euro-aires, but surely they've more than two pairs between them? The ones on the floor, somewhere near Huw's bed where Roddy, or was it Stick, had flung them, smelt like they'd been worn non-stop for a month at least. I mean, gross or what?

And as for their trainers – they reeked! Why is it that other people's daps stink so badly, when your own never seem to even whiff?

And as if that wasn't bad enough, what about the wafts and waves of unmentionable smelliness, bubbling out from under the terrible twins' duvets! I mean, how gross can you get? Who'd have big brothers!

Oh no! Roddy, or was it Stick, was up and out of bed. Coming towards him. Clambering up onto his very own bed (well, Marcus's very own bed, but you know what I mean). Wearing nothing but boxers. Nearly stepping on Huw's face with those pong-a-licious feet – as bad as the socks if not worse. Reaching up to the window, whoever he was. And sliding it shut. Tight shut.

'It's flippin' freezin' in here!' came a smoker's-cough rasp. 'And don't you go opening it again, Marky boy, or I'll have your guts for garters!'

Huw stayed quiet.

'Say you won't, kid, or I'll let one rip in your face, right through me jocks!'

'I won't.'

Oh great, thought Huw. Bloomin' bleedin' great.

He tried to grab a final lungful of outside air but it was too late – its freshness was already fatally contaminated by the proximity of pong-a-licious feet, smoker's-cough breath and the assorted aromas of armpits and worse. Yuk!

*

Huw had never shared a room before. Not with complete strangers, anyway. And he didn't think he liked it, not one little bit.

What was Marcus up to in the camper van, he wondered? Sleeping? Or was he lying awake, tossing and turning, too? Had he come clean to Kath already and given the game away? Or had she spotted some important difference between them, obvious to a mother, even in sleep?

Either way, had his mam kicked poor Marcus out for being an impostor, and was he wandering around Allihies in the dark, not wanting to come into the hostel because he'd have to wake Huw up, and probably Roddy and Stick, too, and then he'd never hear the end of it?

Or maybe, knowing Kath, once she'd got over the surprise, she'd realised it was all a big joke and she and Marcus would be sitting round the table, all cosy warm in their dressing gowns – Huw's dressing gown, in fact – drinking tea and eating chockie bickies and having a good laugh about the whole thing.

Shouldn't he go and join in the fun? Rather than lying here, desperately trying to breathe deeply enough to last out till daybreak, but not deeply enough to inhale the fiendish fumes of feet and farts that filled the room with a ferocious fug?

Or should he just force himself to lie there till morning, try and catch a few precious moments of sleep, and sort it out then?

He was doing well, though, wasn't he? He'd lasted three, no nearly four hours he discovered, checking his mobile phone, without anyone figuring out who he was. Not bad, huh? That's nearly two quid he'd earned already!

Funny sort of family, though. Roddy and Stick couldn't give a monkey's about Marcus, that much was clear. But Huw had thought it'd be tougher to get one past Marcus's mum and da. He'd expected one of them to look in on him, to check their dearly beloved youngest son was safely tucked up in bed.

That's what Kath would have done, for sure. She did it every night, so far as he knew – peeped in to check he was OK, or asleep, or coming to the end of the chapter. Sometimes she'd stop for a chat and it was the best of times, just him and her in the darkness. She'd sit on the side of the bed, when one or other of them had something on their mind, something they really wanted to get off their chest but could only be said when the day was over and the night hadn't quite taken hold.

Yeah, funny sort of family, these O'Malleys, thought Huw. Not like how he thought big families would be, not one little bit. Loads of them, there were, but they weren't all that close, really. Not close like him and Kath, anyway.

Oh for goodness sake, try and get some sleep, boy. You'll need to be bright and breezy in the morning, if you're going to have any chance of keeping this particular game going in the clear light of day.

Talking. That'd be the problem, Huw thought. Keeping up the Irish accent. Using the right words. Not saying anything that betrayed his Welshness. Or anything that showed he didn't know all the ins and outs of Marcus's life and all the little ways he had of going about things – all the things that Marcus's family were much more likely to expect, and notice if they weren't there, than Huw, who'd only known him for a couple of days.

Crazy idea, this, trying to pass yourself off as somebody else. OK if you're a fully-trained-up spy, maybe. Liable to lead to all sorts of complications, too, whenever the truth was uncovered.

And then he had a brainwave. Pretend you've lost your voice in the night, Huw bach! Cough. Whisper. Keep your distance from everyone, as though you're trying to avoid spreading some sort of a sore-throat bug.

You won't have to speak. You won't have to do much at all. You're bound to last out longer than Marcus, 'cos you and Kath – you know each other's little ways back to front, and there's no way that kid's going to last ten minutes pretending to be you. Not once daylight's dawned and Kath's unstuck her sticky eyelids and had her two cups of strong coffee, anyway.

Mightn't be much fun, Huw admitted to himself – pretending to be sick when he should be enjoying the last couple of days of his holiday. But at least he'd be sure to win the bet and all that lovely dosh. And that's what counts, isn't it, Huwie boy?

10

Banjaxed

Dublin Ferryport, Ireland

'Huw?'

'Huh?'

'Wake up!'

'Huh?'

'Are you alive back there? Come on, we've arrived.'

'Arrived? Where?'

'At the ferryport.'

'HUH?'

'I'm sorry, babes.' Kath was concentrating on the delicate manoeuvres needed to board a bus on a boat. 'I didn't want to wake you earlier. Your nain's not well . . .'

'My what?'

'Your nain! Your granny, silly. Wake up, Huw. I need you to help me. She's had a bad fall. She's in hospital, up in Liverpool. I've got to get there, as soon as possible.'

'But . . .'

'But nothing, Huw. Yes, I know we weren't due to leave till tomorrow, but I'd no choice. Surely you understand.'

'But . . .'

'Don't be difficult, love. I know you're still a bit sleepy, but just get yourself dressed and come up on deck with me, there's a good lad.'

'But . . . where are we?'

'We're in Dublin, Huw. We're on the boat.'

'DUBLIN?'

'Yeah, it made more sense than going all the way round by Rosslare. And the ferry company were perfectly happy to let me change the tickets. Now, hurry up, bach. She'll be sailing any minute, and no one's allowed down on the car decks once we've left port.'

*

What to do, when you fall asleep in West Cork and wake up halfway to Wales? When you close your eyes, Marcus O'Malley, the fourth of five from Skerries, County Dublin, and open them to find that you're Huw Davies, only child of an only parent, from deepest darkest Wales?

When you thought you were having a bit of a laugh, a sort of a happy holiday experiment, only to find yourself in the middle of somebody else's real-life disaster – somebody who's so distracted with worry that she doesn't even look at you properly, doesn't pick up on the doubt in your answers.

Do you jump ship and head home to Skerries – I mean, it's only twenty miles or so – and play *Home Alone* till your folks return? No way – poor Kath'd go up the wall if her only beloved son, which is what she thinks you are, suddenly disappeared.

Well, do you tell her what's happened, then, and only add to her worries? Do you come clean, and have to suffer the embarrassment of admitting that you crept into somebody else's camper van – somebody else's bed – under false pretences?

And what happens then? Does she call the police? Do they stop the boat from sailing? Do they track down your ma and da, and drag them all the way back across Ireland to reclaim you? And what sort of a mood'll they be in by the time they get there – spitting blood, for sure!

And what about Roddy and Stick, and Princess Leah, for goodness sake? They'll never let you live it down. Goody-two-shoes, the little bookworm, arrested for trying to pass himself off as someone else! Their family holiday ruined! The sheer total embarrassment of it all! Sure, it'll probably be in the papers, maybe even on the RTÉ news. Everyone in school'll get to hear about it. I mean, talk about a coppertop with a reddener – poor old yours truly'll be blushing himself stupid for the next six months.

And if you do come clean, as you know you really ought to – I mean, isn't honesty just about always the best policy, even when it hurts? – doesn't it make it harder, much harder, for Kath, because all she really cares about at this particular moment in time is being with her mum? Who might be seriously ill, for all you know?

Might even be dying.

Yes, what right have you, Marcus O'Malley, to add a whole load of extra stress on that poor woman, when she's already up to her eyes in worry? What right have you to stand in the way of a daughter being with her mother at a time like this?

Well, what would you do, dear reader? I know what Marcus did. He did nothing.

Nothing except throw on his clothes (Huw's clothes), grab a library book to hide behind if things got difficult (Huw's library book), and head up on deck behind Kath (Huw's mum), who didn't for one minute doubt that the boy shuffling along behind her, his head bowed in confusion and embarrassment, was any other than her one-and-only son.

*

'I've rung Ceri, love.' Kath was striding up the steps ahead of him.

'Ceri?'

'Yeah, you know. I've told you about her. She lives in Aber. Works in the nursery, sometimes. Gareth, her son, is starting at Pendinas on Monday, same as you. She says you can stay with her till I'm back from sorting Mum out.'

'But . . .'

'I'll put you on the train at Holyhead. Ceri'll meet you at Mach, pick up your uniform and schoolbag and stuff from the house, and then drive you to her place.'

'Yeah, but . . .'

'I'm sorry, pet. I know this is difficult for you. I know it's a really big deal, your first day in secondary. But there's nothing else we can do, not with all this business about Mum. It was so kind of Ceri to offer to put you up, and she lives just over the road from the school. And it's not as though you're really nervous about the move – I mean, you said yourself how much you're looking forward to it.'

'Did I?'

'Oh, come on, Huw, you know you did. And Alice'll be there, and you've always got on really well with her, haven't you?'

Silence.

'Well, haven't you?'

'Mmm . . . yeah . . . but . . .'

'She'll probably be in your class.'

'Mmm . . .'

'Look, I know you haven't had the chance to meet Ceri and Gareth yet, so I can understand that it's not exactly ideal, love. I wouldn't do this if I didn't have to, but I've no choice. Surely you can see that?'

'Mmm . . .'

'You'll get on like a house on fire. Ceri's lovely, and Gareth's really nice, too. And they all talk Welsh at home, so it'll be really good for you.'

'But . . .'

'Stop all the ums and buts, Huw!' said Kath, losing patience. 'There's times when you've just got to go along with things, whether you like it or not. I mean, have you a better plan?'

And Marcus, though he'd never met her before, could see that even though Huw's mum was looking him straight in the face now, she wasn't actually looking at him at all, not with the full use of her brain.

He could see her, though – clear as daylight. And he didn't need to actually know her to be able to read the worry in her face – to see that she was so upset about her mother that she couldn't even see that her own son, right there before her was, in actual fact, an impostor.

Not so surprising, though, is it? If somebody looks like somebody, and you've no good reason to think it might be anybody other than that somebody, then the somebody you see is the somebody you think you're seeing, whether they are or not. If you get my drift.

'This isn't like you, Huw,' said Kath, and he could see the tears welling up in her eyes. 'We're family, for heaven's sake. We've got to pull together at a time like this. Agreed?'

She pulled him towards her and hugged him, her whole body heaving as she held him close. And Marcus knew there was no way he could bring himself to tell her, not now. And that he couldn't jump ship before they pulled out of Dublin Ferryport, either.

I'm banjaxed, he thought, surrendering to the hug. Completely one hundred per cent banjaxed.

11

Cornflakes and Fakery

Allihies, County Cork, Ireland

'Howya, Marcus!'

'Oh, eh . . . howya, Daisy!'

'Can you reach me down the cornflakes?'

'Yeah, sure.' Cough. Cough. 'Eh, which cupboard are they in? Oh, here y'are.' Cough. Cough. I should have stayed in bed, thought Huw, to show them what a sore throat I have, so I wouldn't have to talk to anyone. Only I couldn't, he thought. Not one second longer. Not in that ferocious fug.

Daisy poured the milk and started eating. Every now and again, though, she looked up from her bowl.

'Marcus?'

'Yeah.'

'Have you done something funny to your face?'

'No,' Huw muttered into his cereal. 'Must be the way I slept. Not feeling too good.' Cough. Cough.

Daisy munched on. 'Marcus?'

'Yeah?' In a whisper, this time.

'Are you putting on a funny voice or something?'

'No. I mean, yeah. My throat's killing me.'

Cough. Cough.

*

'Hiya, Marcus. Hiya, Daisy.'

'Oh, hiya, Seamus.'

'Ah, I know what it is . . .' said the hostel owner, coming up close to Huw. 'That fella last night, the one singing in Welsh. I knew there was something about him. He's the spitting image of you!'

'Yeah,' piped up Daisy. 'That's Huw! Him and our Marcus are like peas in a pod, aren't they, Seamus? I was the first to notice it. Huw's nice, isn't he?'

'Fine pair of lungs on him, anyway. Bryn Terfel, watch your back, that's what I say.' Seamus was emptying out the bins. 'I love it when the young people sing. That Sorks is a star, don't you think, Marcus?'

He was looking at him again, Huw thought. Surely he hadn't been rumbled already. 'Mmm,' he grunted, nodding into his cornflakes.

'Not too chatty this morning, that brother of yours,' said Seamus, smiling over at Daisy. 'Late night, was it, Marcus? Took your time seeing your young woman home, did you?'

Daisy glanced over at Marcus, a surprised look on her face.

'Don't worry,' said Seamus, tapping his nose. 'I'll keep it to myself, son.'

What's he on about? thought Huw.

And then he got it. Sorcha . . . Marcus . . . the dare. Marcus must have gone ahead with it – sat by her, chatted with her, whatever . . . Seamus must have seen them.

Marcus must have got off with her! Well he's a fly one, and no mistaking. But how come he'd never mentioned it, when they'd met up after? Something to hide, huh?

Huw realised Seamus was still waiting for an

answer to his question. He pointed at his throat, opened his mouth and stuck out his tongue.

'He's got a sore throat,' Daisy explained. 'Can't speak.'

'Ah,' said Seamus, winking at him. 'Fair play to you, boy. Them that can't talk can't be answering any awkward questions.'

And out he went.

*

'Morning, Marcus. Morning, Daisy.'

'Howya, Ma.' Daisy jumped up and gave her mother a hug.

Huw just smiled, weakly. Then pointed his index finger down his open mouth, in the hope of keeping the woman at a distance.

'Toothache?' said Marcus's mother, sympathetically. 'Ah, you poor scrap.'

Huw shook his head.

'Sore throat, then?' she said, coming up to him and ruffling his hair. 'I'm surprised you managed to eat a whole big bowl of cornflakes, though,' she said, looking down at his almost-empty bowl. 'I would've thought they'd be a bit rough on the back of the old voice-box. I'd have made you up some porridge, if you'd only asked. Slips down much easier.'

'I love porridge, Mammy,' said Daisy. 'You hardly ever make it at home!'

Her mother sighed. 'Sure, you know there's nothing I'd like more than to stand around in the kitchen of a morning, making porridge and baking bread, Daisy love. But there's never enough hours in the day. It's always such a mad rush to get everyone up and out, never mind myself . . .'

Huw sighed. Caught out on the cornflakes! I'm rubbish at this, he thought. I've just not been brought up to be a good liar. That Kath's got a lot to answer for.

He looked at Daisy. She was staring at him again, with an even more quizzical look on her face. I'd better get the heck out of here, he thought, or I haven't a hope in hell of lasting more than five minutes.

12

Abracadabra

Machynlleth, Powys, Wales

'Shwmai, Huw?'

'Huh?'

'Ceri ydw i. Ffrind dy fam.'

'What?'

Gareth was watching him. 'I've a feeling he doesn't actually speak much Welsh, Mam. Do you, Huw?'

'Eh no, not a lot.'

'But I thought . . .' Ceri was flustered. 'Kath told me . . . Oh well, never mind. I'm Ceri and this is Gareth.'

'Hi. I'm, eh . . . Huw – Huw Davies,' said Marcus, holding out his hand. 'My mam, I mean, eh . . . Kath told me about you. Have you come to take me to Abracada . . . eh . . .?' Damn. The name of that town they lived in was such a mouthful, he couldn't even remember how to say it. Definitely not Abracadabra, though – it was more of a spelling-test than a spell.

'We have, yeah,' said Ceri, taking hold of the hand he was offering and shaking it in return. He had a slight feeling, though, that it wasn't what she'd expected. And when he offered his hand to Gareth, the other boy frowned, then giggled, then shook, in an embarrassed sort of a way. Hmm, thought Marcus – must be another difference between Ireland and Wales. He could see they thought he was a bit weird, but at least they didn't appear to suspect that he was anyone other than who he was pretending to be.

'We just need to stop off at your place first and pick up whatever you need,' said Gareth's mother. 'I'm sorry to hear about your nain, Huw.'

My nine? Marcus frowned. Oh yeah, my granny.

'I hope she'll be all right,' the woman went on. 'It must be a terrible worry for you both.'

'Yeah. It must . . . I mean, it is. Thanks for helping out, Mrs . . . eh . . .'

'Ceri.'

'Yeah, thanks for helping out, Mrs Kerry.'

'No!' The woman and her son both laughed. 'Ceri's my first name. Ceri Richards.'

'Yeah, and I'm Gareth Richards,' said her son.

'Oh, right . . . sorry,' said Marcus, all of a fluster. 'Well thanks, anyway. You've been really kind to take me in.'

'No problem, bach. That's what friends are for, isn't it?'

*

Right. 1 Penrallt Street. He'd checked in Kath's wallet.

'It's OK. You don't need to tell me how to find it,' said Ceri, at the wheel. 'I've popped in for a coffee with your mam after work a couple of times.'

Luckily Kath had given him the key, and the number was on the door. He'd have looked pretty stupid not even knowing which house he lived in.

Ceri and Gareth waited outside in the van while Marcus let himself in. Then he rummaged around, looking for Huw's schoolbag and uniform and stuff.

He eventually found them all hanging tidily together in the wardrobe and the satchel, ready packed, was on the top of the chest of drawers. I'd better grab a few extra clothes, he thought. No knowing how long I'll be there.

Funny house, this. Tiny rooms. You can tell they haven't much money. I mean look at these clothes! And where does Huw keep his telly and computer? Don't tell me he has to share the one downstairs.

Sort of cosy, though, Marcus thought, looking round. Friendly sort of a feel about it.

A cat came up the stairs, mewing. It took one look at him and stopped dead.

'I know,' said Marcus, not in the least bit surprised to be outed by a dumb animal. 'I'm sorry, puss,' he said, leaning down and stroking it. 'I hope someone's feeding you.'

He left a note by the cat food, just in case.

> *Emergency. Had to rush away again.*
> *Please buy some more cat food, and I'll*
> *sort it out with you when I get back.*
> *Thanks a million,*
> *Kath.*

That sounds about right, thought Marcus. Probably nothing like her writing, but it's the best I can do.

13

Daisy, Detective

Allihies, County Cork, Ireland

'Huw! Wait for me!'

He turned round at the sound of his name, only to find Daisy, running after him as he headed off down to the beach.

'Hah!' she cried. 'Caught you out! I knew you weren't Marcus!'

Damn. He'd been rumbled.

'Where's my brother, Huw? What have you done with him?'

'Ah, don't worry, Daisy. It's just a wee game we've been playing,' said Huw, trying to keep up the Irish accent. It was easier with nobody else about – just try and sound like Daisy.

'What game?' she cried. 'I want to play!'

'It's a secret,' said Huw. 'Keep your voice down.'

'I'm really good at secrets,' whispered Daisy. 'I know lots of them.'

'Like what?' Huw asked her.

And Daisy was just about to tell him one, when she realised that this time it was him playing the trick. 'I can't tell you,' she said, giving him a little I-know-your-game sort of a look. 'They're secret! But if you tell me where my brother is, I promise I won't let anyone else know. Please tell me. Please!'

'OK,' said Huw, taking pity on her. 'Marcus and me – we've done a swap.'

'A swap? 'Cos you're so alike? That's cool!'

'Yeah, it is, isn't it? I'm staying up at the hostel, pretending to be him, and he's down on the campsite, being me.'

'Where? In a tent?'

'No, the Turtle. We've got a camper van, see. He'll be in there with Kath – my mam.'

'Your mammy? And she'll be thinking he's you? That's deadly!'

'Well, maybe. It depends on how wide awake she is.'

'You swapped clothes?' Daisy was looking him up and down.

'Yeah. Feels a bit weird.'

'You look really like him,' she said, admiringly. 'Even more than you usually do.'

'The perfect spit?'

'The perfect PERFECT spit!'

'Thanks, Daisy. Not good enough to fool you, though. So how did you know, anyway?'

'Know what?'

'That it was me – Huw?'

'Oh, I could just tell. You can't mistake your own brother!'

'Roddy and Stick did.'

'Yeah, well . . . Did you kip in their room?'

Huw nodded.

'That's cool!' said Daisy. 'What was it like? I bet it was minging.'

'It was stinking,' Huw agreed.

Daisy laughed. 'But did you see how Seamus didn't recognize you? And then me ma?' Her smile turned to a frown. 'How come she didn't even notice?'

'Well, you did say we look nearly the same.'

'Yeah, but really – her own son! So are you going to pretend to be Marcus to your own mammy?'

'How do you mean?'

'When we get to the van? Are you going to say "Hello, Mrs . . ." whatever your name is.'

'Davies.'

'Yeah, are you going to knock, and if she comes to the door, are you going to say "Hello, Mrs Davies. Is Huw there? I've just come to play"?'

'Do you think I should, Daisy?'

'Yeah, it'll be a laugh. I'll be your little sister, so I'll tell you what to do. You've got to say, "I'm Marcus, and this is my little sister, Daisy. We've come to play with Huw. Is he in, Mrs?" Go on, let me hear you.'

'All right,' Huw sighed. 'I'm Marcus,' he repeated, 'and this is my little sister, Daisy.' He could hardly say it for giggles, and Daisy was all crumpled up with laughter. 'We've come to play with Huw. Is he in, Mrs Davies?'

'You don't sound a bit like Marcus,' said Daisy, frowning.

'Don't I?' Huw was disappointed. He'd been putting on his best Irish accent. 'But then, my mother's never met Marcus before,' he told her, 'so she won't know how he talks, anyway.'

'You're right!' Daisy clapped her hands. 'It'll be the best laugh! Now, try it again. I'll be your mammy, this time.'

'Knock, knock,' said Huw.

'Squeeeeak,' went Daisy.

'Good morning, Mrs Davies,' said Huw. 'I'm sorry to disturb you so early, but is Huw in? I've come to play.'

'Certainly, young man. I'll go and tell him you're here,' said Daisy. 'Who'll I say is calling?'

'Huw . . . I mean, eh, Marcus. It's his friend, Marcus.'

'Marcus? I didn't know he'd a friend called Marcus.'

'Oh, we met down by the harbour yesterday.'

'Mmm . . .' Daisy sounded unconvinced. 'Haven't I seen you somewhere before, Marcus?'

'No . . . eh, no, I don't think so,' said Huw, trying to hide his face behind his hand. 'Just get on and tell him, Daisy, will you?'

'That's a bit rude!' said Daisy.

'Well, you're making it difficult,' Huw

complained. 'Kath wouldn't leave one of my friends standing on the doorstep, like that. She'd invite them in.'

'Right,' said Daisy, ushering him past her. 'Come on in, Marcus. Make yourself comfortable and I'll go and find him for you. He's probably reading a book . . .'

'Brilliant!' said Huw. 'Let's try it. But you're not to giggle when we get to the van, Daisy, or you'll give the game away.'

'Cross my heart and hope to die.'

'We'd better just check Marcus isn't up and about yet, before we go banging on the door,' Huw told her.

They had a look on the beach, but there was no one there, only some man, over by the rocks, looking out to sea through binoculars.

'No sign of him,' said Huw. 'Let's go and check the Turtle, then. Here we go.'

Daisy slipped her hand into his. She couldn't hold back the giggles.

'And no giggling,' he told her. 'Or I'll identi-tickle you!'

'Hey, Huw,' said Daisy. 'You're a howl.'

'Yeah, well you're a caterwaul,' said Huw.

'What the heck's that?' she giggled. 'A cat on a wall?'

'You should know,' he said. 'Seeing it's you . . .'

'You're mad, Huw,' said Daisy.

'Fair dos,' said Huw. 'But you're chopsy – I'll tell you that for nothing.'

'Chopsy?' said Daisy, delighted with the insult though she hadn't a clue what it meant. 'Well, you're steak and kidney!'

*

'What's the matter, Huw?' He'd gone all quiet. 'What's wrong?'

'It's just . . . The van . . . It was here . . .'

'Where?'

'Here. Right here.' He pointed to the ground. 'Look – you can see the tyre marks. And here, where we had a barbecue.'

'Has she moved it, Huw? Maybe they wanted to get closer to the sea?'

But there was no sign of it anywhere.

'They've gone!' cried Huw. 'They've gone in the night!'

'And left you here?' said Daisy, wide-eyed. 'Your mammy's gone and left you?' And then she realised what else that meant. 'Marcus!' she moaned. 'She's taken our Marcus with her!'

'No,' gasped Huw. 'She can't have!'

*

The man with the binoculars was standing by one of the tents.

'That old VW camper . . .' said Huw. 'Did you see what happened to it?'

'I did not,' said the man, crossly. 'But I heard it, all right. Revving up and driving off in the middle of the night, waking everyone up. They didn't look the type to go disturbing everyone's sleep like that . . .'

And then he took a closer look at Huw. 'Hey, you're the boy from the van – I thought you'd have gone with her. Where's your mother got to, anyway? I'll be having a word with her when she's back and no mistaking.'

'Me too,' muttered Huw, as the man marched off in disgust.

Daisy took a hold of Huw's hand again and gave it a tight little squeeze. 'I think you'd better come back to our place,' she said.

'Kath's right,' said Huw, as they headed back up the road to the hostel. 'Be careful what you wish for, she always said.'

14

Twpsyn

'You're quiet, Huw? Are you all right?'

'It's all right, Mam. Leave him be. He's probably worried about his nain.'

'Of course he is. Sorry, bach.'

They pulled into the driveway.

'I'll show you your room.' Gareth led Marcus up the stairs and threw open a door.

'It's nice,' said Marcus. 'Thanks.'

'I'll leave you to it, then.'

'Yeah, thanks.'

But Gareth didn't go. He crossed the room and stood by the window. 'Just think,' he said, pointing at the building across the road. 'Monday morning we'll be in there, finding out what class we're in and what teachers we're getting. Don't know about you, but I'm scared stiff.'

Marcus looked. And looked again. 'That's the school?' It was enormous.

'Yeah.' Gareth gave him a funny look. 'You came for the open day, didn't you?'

'Eh, yeah. It just looks . . . bigger from here.'

'Oh, that's only part of it. There's over fourteen hundred pupils, Mam told me. Two hundred and fifty in year seven!'

'So how many are there in the first year?' Marcus asked him.

'That is the first year, you twp!'

Year seven's year one? Oh dear, thought Marcus. Keep your big mouth shut – you're being an eejit again. Or a 'toop', whatever that is.

He sat himself on the edge of the bed.

'Come down when you're ready,' said Gareth, seeing his visitor look a little flushed. 'We can go take a walk down into town.'

*

Marcus got his mobile out. Checked his messages.

'Where r u?' said one from Huw. 'Wot's happening? Kath's not answering.'

Marcus thought he'd better ring him.

'Marcus!' Huw picked up the phone straight away. 'Where the hell are you? What have you done with Kath? I tried ringing her mobile, but she's not answering.'

'I'm in Aberwhisswiss, or whatever you call it . . .'

'You're in Aber! What the hell are you doing in Aber?'

'I'm staying at Gareth's?'

'Who the heck's Gareth?'

'He's . . .'

*

'I've made us a cup of tea, Huw. Do you want me to bring it up to you?' It was Ceri, peeping her head round the door. 'Oh, sorry, bach, you're on the phone.'

'It's all right. I'll be down in a minute.'

*

'Who was that?' Huw asked him.

'Ceri,' said Marcus.

'Ceri?'

'She's a friend of your ma's. Of Kath's.'

'How come you know friends of my mam that I don't even know?'

'It's a long story.'

'Just tell me this, Marcus – why did you up and leave in the middle of the night? And what the hell have you done with my mother? It isn't funny anymore, you know.'

'What's she done with me, more like. Look, Huw, do you think I want to be here in Aberwhatjamacallit with a load of people I've never met before? Going to some sort of a school that looks more like a prison? So you needn't think it's a bundle of laughs this end, either. And it wasn't just my idea, this changing places thing; it was yours, too, remember.'

'Yeah, OK. Keep your hair on, Marcus. I just didn't realise you were gonna up and desert me as soon as my back was turned. I mean how would you feel if your only family abandoned you hundreds of miles from home?'

'Much like I do now!'

'Yeah, maybe. Anyway, tell me what happened.'

'Kath got a call to say your gran – your 'eight', or whatever you call her . . .'

'Nain, y'eejit! She's my nain!'

'Yeah, your nine. Well . . . I'm sorry, but she's had some sort of a bad fall. She's been taken to hospital in Liverpool or somewhere. Your ma – I mean, your mam's gone to be with her.'

'Nain? How is she?'

'I don't know, I'm afraid. All I do know is your ma's left me here in Aberwhisswiss, or whatever you call it, with a bunch of Welshies.'

'Welsh speakers?'

'Yeah. Ceri's some friend of hers from work. Her son, Gareth, starts at this massive great factory of a school just across the road on Monday, same as you . . . I mean me. It's terrifying! I'm not supposed to start big school for another year!'

'Hah!'

'Hah what?'

'It sounds like you got more than you bargained for, Marcus O'Malley. Serves you right for upping and leaving without saying a word. But at least you won the bet. I must owe you loads of money – not that I've got any.'

'You've been found out already?'

''Fraid so. It was Daisy worked it out. Mind you, I don't think anyone else round here's all that bothered who I am, to tell you the truth. Not anyone in your family, anyway.'

'You're spot on there, kid.'

'So Kath's in Liverpool?'

'Or, where was it, Chess-something,' replied Marcus.

'Chester? Yeah, that's where my nain lives.'

'That's it, then. She fell off her bike and broke her arm. Hit her head, too. She's having tests.'

'That's terrible! I bet she wasn't wearing a helmet, either.'

'No. I don't think she was.'

'I tell her every time I see her!' exclaimed Huw. 'Right. I'll ring the hospital. See if I can find out what's going on, and track down Kath, too.'

'Good idea.'

'So do you want me to tell your folks where you are?'

'Suppose you'd better. Shouldn't think they care, anyway.'

'Daisy cares.'

'I guess that's better than nothing.'

'The others are all so busy, I hardly see them.'

'That figures. They're a right shower. What was it like sleeping with Roddy and Stick, by the way?'

'Minging! Why's Stick called Stick, anyway?'

'It's what we've always called him.'

'Weird name, though . . .'

'His real name's Stewart. Roddy couldn't say it properly when he was little, so he called him Stick instead.'

'And it stuck?'

'Yeah,' Marcus laughed.

'Anyway, I'd better go – this call'll be costing me a fortune. Good luck at school, if you get there before this thing's sorted.'

'And you.'

'No mitching, now.'

'Huh?'

'Skiving off. Don't do it.'

'I won't.'

'Hey, Huw . . .'

'Yeah.'

'I know I was whinging on a bit, just then, but I'm actually quite enjoying this, in a funny sort of way.'

'Are you?'

'Yeah. It's, like, a challenge.'

'Hmm.'

'You know what?' said Marcus.

'What?'

'Even though I'm not too keen on the look of that school of yours, I actually wouldn't mind this thing going on a bit longer.'

'You wouldn't?'

'No.'

'Oh. Right.'

'Hey, Huw?'

'Yeah?'

'What's a 'toop'?'

'A what?'

'A 'toop'. Gareth called me one.'

'Ah. A twp!'

'That's what I said, you duh. So, what does it mean?'

'It's short for twpsyn.'

'"Toopsin?"'

'Yeah. It means eejit.'

'Oh, right.'

So Marcus, aka Huw, headed down for tea, Welsh cakes and bara brith.

Two small countries, he thought. So many differences.

15

Bad News, Babes

Allihies, County Cork, Ireland

'Kath?' She'd answered the phone at last!

'Huw? Is that you?'

'How are you?'

'I'm fine, babes. But your nain's not at all well. I'm going to have to stay with her here a few more days.'

'Did she fracture her skull?'

'No, love. A load of stitches, but they want to keep her here a while longer, just to be sure she's all right. She's a sprightly old bird, as you know, but she's no spring chicken. What with cracking her head open – that and the broken arm – she's in a bit of a mess, I'm afraid. These things can really take it out of you at her age. So I might have to stay at her place with her for a few days, once they let her out, just to settle her in. I'm sorry, Huw. It's dreadful timing.'

'It's OK,' said Huw. 'I'll be all right.'

'How are things there? Are Ceri and Gareth being nice to you? Are you still looking forward to school?'

'Eh, yeah. It's fine. Everything's fine.' What else could he say? If he told her she'd left him in Ireland, she'd be frantic.

'Sorry, pet,' said Kath. 'I've got to go.' Huw could hear his nain, muttering in the background. 'I'll ring you later.'

'Oh, OK. Love you.'

'Love you too, bach. Look after yourself. And good luck on Monday.'

'Monday?'

'School,' she reminded him.

'Oh yeah. Thanks.'

What good would it do, telling her what's happened? thought Huw. It'd only add to her worries. And I couldn't go home anyway, 'cos there's nobody there. I'd only end up at Ceri and Gareth's, whoever they are. And it'd be so much hassle getting there – they'd never let me travel on my own, so one of Marcus's parents would have to come with me. Or the police or something. And would they be happy to let me stay with complete strangers? Somehow I don't think so. They'd call in the social workers. Put me in some sort of care home. Kath'd get into all sorts of trouble . . .

Oh, stuff it. I'll stay here a while longer. It's not too bad, I suppose – apart from having to hold your breath all night 'cos of Roddy and Stick. I'll see if I can get Daisy to help. Play the game a bit longer. Have some fun, like me and Marcus planned.

*

'Hey, Daisy.'

She stopped the swing. 'Yeah?'

'New plan.'

'Howd'ya mean?'

'We're not going to tell your folks – not for a while longer, anyway.'

'We're not?'

'No. Not till things settle down at home a bit.'

'Why?'

''Cos it'd only upset everyone. And it wouldn't do them any good right now.'

'You sure?'

'Yeah, I'm sure.'

'What about Marcus?' Daisy asked.

'I spoke to him. He's happy to stay in Wales a few more days.'

'He is?'

'Yeah.'

'Isn't he scared?' Daisy asked him.

'Scared?'

'Yeah. He's a bit shy sometimes, you know.'

'I noticed,' said Huw. 'Especially with girls. But he sees it as a challenge. He's decided to see how brave he can be.'

'Like the lion?' suggested Daisy.

'The lion?'

'Yeah. In *The Wizard of Oz*.'

'Yeah,' Huw nodded. 'Like the lion.'

'What about your ma?' Daisy asked. 'Doesn't she want you back?'

'She's stuck in Liverpool with my nain.'

'Your what?'

'My granny. So I might as well stay here for a while.'

'Pretending to be Marcus?'

'Yeah. Will you help me, Daisy?'

She had a think about it. Then she ran and threw her arms around his legs. 'It'll be deadly, Huw!'

'Who?' Huw frowned down at her.

'Marcus, then. But I like your real name better,' said Daisy, giggling. 'It makes you sound like an owl.'

'What does?'

'Huw,' she said. 'Too-whit, too-huw.'

'Two Huws,' said Huw. 'The twinnies!'

'The perfect spit,' said Daisy, giggling.

'But that's the last time you call me Huw,' he said, looking stern. 'From now on I'm Marcus – your brother, OK?'

'OK, OK. Keep your hair on, Huw.'

He gave her an even sterner look.

'Sorry . . . Marcus.' She smiled. 'And don't worry. I won't let the caterwaul out of the bag.'

'I've a sore throat, remember,' Huw told her. 'So I don't have to talk much.'

'Okey dokey, croaky owl,' said Daisy, with a laugh. And she jumped off the swing, took him by the hand and skipped him back to the hostel.

'You're gas, you know,' she said, with a happy little chuckle.

'Yeah, well you're electricity,' said Huw.

16

Aberwhisswiss

Aberystwyth, Ceredigion, Wales

'Where are you off to?' Ceri asked them.

'Just down the town, Mam.'

'Show young Huw the bright lights, is it?'

'Yeah, sort of . . .'

'Fair dos. Make sure you're home by six, cariad.'

'OK. See you later.'

*

'Steep hill, this,' said Marcus.

'Yeah.' Gareth was striding out ahead of him. 'It's fun going down, but it'll be one hell of a pull back up.'

'I bet.'

'Uni . . . Pantycelyn . . .' Gareth pointed out the landmarks as they went.

'Huh?'

'Halls of residence. Where the Welsh-speaking students live.'

'Oh, right.'

'National Library . . .' said Gareth, coming to a halt.

'It's big!' said Marcus.

'Yeah, it's got a copy of every book that's ever been written, just about.'

'It can't be all the books in the world,' Marcus argued. 'There'd be millions of them.'

'Trillions, I'd say.'

'Gazillions, actually,' said Marcus, 'if it's all the books in every language since the Stone Age.'

'They didn't have books in the Stone Age, you dork.'

'What about the *Flintstones*? That's the Stone Age,' said Marcus, smiling.

'Yeah, but that's telly, not books,' Gareth argued.

'That's where you're wrong,' replied Marcus. 'Haven't you seen the *Flintstones* annuals – we've got a load of them at home. But I suppose you're right. It can't be *all* the books ever published, in any language. It must be just all the ones in English.'

'And in Welsh,' Gareth reminded him. 'It's the National Library of Wales, remember.'

'Yeah, of course.' Careful, Marcus told himself. Just be careful. 'So where do they keep them all?' he asked. 'Just in that building? It'd never be big enough.'

'No, under the ground, they say.'

'All under the hill here, with the cars driving over them?'

'Maybe. And the students tramping up and down, all day, every day. The corridors go on for miles, they say.'

'Maybe, if they go all the way to Mak— to my place, I could dig a big hole in my back garden and go down and borrow them from there,' Marcus suggested. But suddenly ding dong, alarm bells went off in his head. What'd you say that for, y'eejit? Huw hasn't even got a back garden, remember. Hopefully Gareth doesn't know.

He didn't, or he didn't pick up on it, anyway.

'Now you're being dumb again,' said Gareth. 'And

you're not allowed to borrow books from the National Library, anyway. You have to read them there.'

'Funny sort of a library,' said Marcus, 'if you can't take the books home.'

'Yeah. But it's a reading library. That's what they call it.'

'Rather than a . . . whatjamacallit?'

'A lending library. Like the one in town. Suppose you've got one in Mach, have you?'

'Suppose,' said Marcus, shrugging his shoulders.

'What, you don't know?'

'Not really. I just buy books if I want to read them.'

Gareth gave him a look. 'What – are you a millionaire or something?'

'No. Eh . . .' Marcus gave a nervous little laugh. 'Course not.' Change the subject, y'eejit. 'You'd think they'd be squashed flat by now, though, wouldn't you?'

'How do you mean?'

'The books – in the National Library, there. What with all these people walking all over them all the time.'

'Yeah. Or all muddy, being underground, like that.'

'Or rotted away to dust, like dead bodies.'

'Imagine going down to find a book and getting lost,' suggested Gareth.

'Locked in, overnight . . .'

'Haunted by the ghosts of every book that ever lived and died . . .'

'Hey, I just remembered – there's one in Dublin, too, you know,' said Marcus, remembering how Roddy and Stick had teased him ages ago, when they'd just got into the car setting off for Allihies. Only a week or so back, he realised, but it felt like ages. A whole other lifetime, in fact.

'What, a library? Big deal!'

'No. One like that,' he said, pointing, 'with all the books ever written.'

'Ah, but have they got the ones in Welsh?' Gareth asked him.

'No – in English, of course.'

'Then ours is better.'

'No, it's not.'

'Yeah it is. 'Cos ours'll have more books.'

'No, it won't.'

'Yeah, it will. English and Welsh.'

'No, 'cos I bet the one in Dublin's got all the books written in Irish, too.'

'Irish?'

'Yeah. There is an Irish language too, you know!'

'Fair enough, but I bet there aren't nearly as many books in Irish as there are in Welsh. I mean, does anyone speak it?'

'Course they do. They learn it at school. All over Ireland.'

'Yeah, but do they use it at home?' said Gareth. 'Is it their first language, like it is here?'

'Well, some do. Over in the west. And a few others, round Dublin and stuff.'

'Yeah, but I bet there aren't as many as speak Welsh.'

'Bet there is. Ireland's much bigger than Wales.'

'Yeah maybe, but I still say there's more people speak Welsh. It was the first written language in Europe, so they told us in school.'

'Never!'

'Don't they teach you anything up in Machynlleth? I thought you lot up there went on about it being the cultural capital of the nation – Owain Glyndŵr and all that . . . Which I always thought was a stupid idea, anyway. I mean, it's obviously Aberystwyth, not Machynlleth – what with the University and the National Library and . . .'

Marcus hadn't a clue what he was on about, of course, but he tried not to look too dim.

'You'll have a lot of catching up to do at Pendinas, I can see that,' said Gareth. 'Where's this library you know so much about, anyway?'

'At Trinity.'

'What's Trinity?'

'The uni in Dublin, y'eejit!'

Gareth gave him a funny look. 'So how come you know so much about Dublin?'

'Huh?'

'Well, how come you know all about this bloomin' great library in Dublin, that you think's so much better than ours, when you don't even know about the one in Aberystwyth, right on your doorstep? And when you don't even use libraries, anyway, so you tell me.'

'Eh . . .'

'I mean, Dublin's hundreds of miles away. It's in another country, for flip's sake. And you only live just up the road from here.'

'Yeah, well . . . I used to live near Dublin for a while, see.' Well, it's not a lie, thought Marcus. I did. About twenty-four hours or so ago, give or take a holiday in Allihies.

'Really?'

'Yeah. My dad's Irish. That's why I've got red hair and freckles.'

'Yeah, maybe. But there's loads of Welsh people with red hair and freckles, too, you know. Anyway, where's your dad now?'

'He's back there now.' Well he is.

'Oh right . . . sorry.' It was Gareth's turn to be embarrassed. 'Is he coming here? To live with you in Mach, I mean?'

'I shouldn't think so.'

'Shame. Mine scarpered, too.'

'Huh?'

'Ran off with a younger model, according to Mam.'

'How do you mean?'

'Living down Swansea way, the two of them. I just about never see him any more.'

'Oh, right. Must be bad, that.'

'What?'

'Living without one of your parents.'

'Like you, you mean?' Gareth was giving him another funny look.

'Eh, yeah.' Well, I am, thought Marcus. Living without either parent, as a matter of fact. For the time being, anyway. But I'd better not mention that. In fact I think I'd better just shut my big Irish mouth, before I get myself into even deeper water.

*

They carried on their walking. 'Bronglais . . .' said Gareth, pointing out the next big building.

'I wonder why there's an ambulance outside,' said Marcus. 'One of the students must have had an accident.'

'Duh . . .' Gareth made one of his duh faces. 'It's a hospital, stupid.'

'Oh, sorry,' said Marcus. 'I thought it must be another of those student places.'

'Don't you know one single thing about Aberystwyth, Huw? Surely you've been to Bronglais? Haven't you ever broken an arm or something.'

'Eh, no,' said Marcus, shaking his head. 'Never.'

'But surely you've been to Aber, even if you haven't been to the hospital. I mean you must have at least heard of Bronglais. Everyone has!'

'Well, no . . . I mean, not often. I usually hang round at home. And we haven't lived there all that long, really,' he said, taking a risk.

'In Mach?'

'Yeah, Mach,' said Marcus, picking up on the way Gareth said 'ch' but over-stressing it, so a whole load of spit sprayed from his mouth. Mach as in loch, he thought . . . Mach as in loch as in lough as in Neagh.

He was pleased with himself, then. Pleased to find he could make a Welsh sound so successfully. Pleased too to have discovered its nickname, because he knew he'd have no end of trouble saying his supposed home town's complete name properly (never mind trying to remember how to spell it – now that really was a challenge).

And if he couldn't even say it right, it was bound to be the real giveaway, especially at a new school.

*

'What's your name, boy?' he'd imagined some teacher asking, probably in front of the whole class. In fact he'd probably ask it in Welsh, which'd be the real killer.

'Marcus O' . . . eh, Huw, sorry . . . Huw Davies, sir.'

Giggles from the back. A right twpsyn we've got here, they're thinking. Doesn't even know his own name. We'll have some fun with him.

'And where are you from, Marcus O'Huw?'

More giggles.

'Sker . . . no, eh . . . Mack . . . I'm from Mack, sir.'

'Makser? Is that Ceredigion, Powys or Gwynedd?'

'Huh? Eh, no, eh, Machun . . .' Remember to huch, nice and throat-clearly. Don't worry if it sends a fine spray all over your brand new teacher's leering grin. It'll shut him up, the bully-of-new-boys that he is.

'Machynlleth, do you mean, boy? You don't seem too sure where you come from.'

'Yeah, that's it, sir. That's the place, exactly.'

Hopeless. He'd be found out in five minutes flat. I mean, Aberwhisswiss was bad enough, but

Machynlleth! How are you supposed to know how to pronounce a word like that, when it's at home? thought Marcus, as the grumpy old teacher added it to the list on the board:

'Huw Davies, Machynlleth,' he wrote.

All 'y's and 'l's and hardly a vowel in sight, thought Marcus, copying it down in his homework book. Eleven letters and only one 'a' and one 'e' – surely that's a bit stingy on the vowel count, isn't it?

I mean, back home, we've got Irish names for things, he was thinking, as the teacher carried on interrogating the class. But we don't all call it Baile Átha Cliath, do we? We call it Dublin. Much easier on the vocal chords, and the tourists. So why's that then?

Hmmm. Maybe it's what Gareth was saying about people actually using the language more. Maybe it's 'cos Irish is a second language to most Irish people in Dublin, whereas Welsh is a first language to most Welsh people round here. Could that be it?

Anyway, 'Machynlleth', he mouthed, over and over to try to fix it in his head.

He'd been trying to work out how to say it ever

since he'd seen it on the train ticket Kath had given him, before she disappeared out of his life almost as fast as she'd come in. But, no matter how hard he tried, it never sounded right. Ma-chin-lit. Mak-yin-let, he'd been saying. Weird language, this Welsh. Not like Irish at all. Which is odd, considering they're only over the water from one another. And they're supposed to be related, aren't they? (Irish and Welsh, that is. Not Huw and Marcus. Or Gareth.) Not quite identi-tickle, not quite the perfect spit, but first cousins at least.

In fact the name of his supposed home town had only started to make sense as a word once he'd twigged from Gareth that the Welsh ch is like the Irish gh – Mach as in loch as in lough as in Neagh. Sort of.

*

'OK, OK, no need to splatter me,' said Gareth, getting a neck full of uchs, as he practised.

'Sorry,' said Marcus, switching towns. 'Aber, Aber, Aber . . .' he muttered under his breath, striding down the hill behind his new-found friend. Maybe when I get to school, I'll pretend I'm from here instead, just to be on the safe side. Can't go wrong with Aber, he thought – heck of a lot easier to say, for sure.

*

Down past the shops to the seafront.

Wasting a load of money in the arcade. Finding out which machines'll accept all those spare euros jangling about in your pocket. Bargain! Cheap at half the price!

Even more of a bargain when Marcus discovered, by mistake of course, that you could stick a twenty cent coin into the one pound slot of a change machine – well, you could in this one – and make a tidy profit every time! Whoopy doopy, keep it secret.

Down onto the jetty, then, playing chicken with the sea.

'My daps!' cries Gareth, staring at his soggy trainers. 'They'd better be dry by the time we get home or Mam'll be tamping!'

Tamping? Daps? What sort of English is that? Welsh English? English Welsh? Makey-uppy?

Walking along the sand till it turns to pebbles.

Picking up a few thin flat ones and having a go at skimming. Fiercely contested competition, it turns out to be. You can tell you've both been brought up living by the sea. Except you haven't, of course, 'cos you're supposed to be Huw, not Marcus. You're supposed to be from Mach, spit, spit, not Aber. Better let Gareth win, then, or he'll be wondering how you got so good.

Fifteen jumps! Wow!

Up onto the prom and all the way along to the big massive hill at the end. Consti, Gareth calls it. Funny name for a hill. Sounds more like a small guard (or a baby policeman, as they call them over here, he'd realised).

Hell of a pull to the top, as Gareth would say, but the view when you get there's amazing, all across the town, up the coast and out to sea.

'Can you see Ireland from here?' you ask, peering into the distance, trying to pick something, anything, out on the distant horizon.

'Shouldn't think so,' comes the response. 'What would you want to see that dump for?'

'Oh, no reason. No reason at all.' Stop going on about Ireland, y'eejit, or you'll be rumbled for sure.

SWAP

Staring out to sea like a washed-up sailor and, talking of rumbles, feeling a lump, deep down in your belly, and realising either one of two things. Either you're deadly doubled-up hungry. Or totally tripled-up homesick.

17

Who's Who?

Allihies, County Cork, Ireland

'More spuds?'

Huw looked up. 'Thanks, Ka . . .'

Daisy shot him a warning glance.

'. . . ree on, Ma,' Huw managed to correct himself, as Marcus's mother spooned another two potatoes onto his plate. A sneaky smile of gratitude to Daisy. Phew, that was a close one.

'Any sign of Roddy and Stick?'

'Haven't seen them all morning, Ma,' said Daisy.

'Your da's gone fishing, love. Leah's out with her young man.'

'Again?' said Daisy.

'Yeah. It must be serious. You're quiet, Marcus. Throat still sore?'

Huw nodded. Gave her a pained expression.

'Meat a bit hard to swallow, love?'

Huw was carefully avoiding the pork chop. Trying, in fact, not to even look at it. Help, he thought! Meat, he thought! How do I tell them I'm a veggie?

'Yeah, sorry, Ma,' he whispered. 'The spuds are lovely.'

'Here, I got you some TCP,' she told him, fetching a bottle from her bag. 'Have a gargle after your lunch.'

Yuk.

And he wished she'd stop looking at him. Even though he wasn't quite as prone to reddening as Marcus, all this attention, on top of his guilty secret, was making him blush something chronic.

'Do you want some paracetamol, love? You look a bit flushed.' Marcus's mother came over and felt his forehead. 'Yes, I'd say you've a temperature, you poor dote. Don't worry about your chop. Just do your gargle and take a couple of these,' she said, handing him two tablets from a box in her bag. 'Then away up to bed with you. I'll tell the boys not to bother you when they come in.'

There was nothing for it, under the attentive gaze

of Mrs O'Malley but to take a swig of the TCP – yuk, how he hated that stuff. Just about bearable, when you think it might do you some good, but when you don't even need it – disgusting!

Round and round in his mouth and then, hoick – the perfect spit – into the sink. Four times. With Daisy trying not to laugh. Then gulping down a glass of water, pretending to take the tablets but in fact hiding them in his hand, and heading out of the room.

Huw had no intention of going to bed, though. As soon as he knew Marcus's ma was out of sight of the front windows, he slipped out of the hostel and headed down to the beach.

*

Sorcha was there, gazing at the sea.

'Hi, Sorks!'

She glanced up. Her eyes sparkled for a split second, and then glazed over.

'Oh hi, Marcus,' she said. 'How ye doing?'

Huw croaked, pointing to his neck.

'Sore throat?' she asked.

He nodded.

'Where's Huw?' Sorcha asked him. 'Did ye see him this morning?'

Huw shrugged.

'I thought he said he'd a camper van down at the site,' said Sorcha.

Huw nodded again.

'There's no sign of one. Do ye know where they're parked up, Marcus? I really need to speak to him.'

'They're gone,' croaked Huw, matter-of-factly.

'Gone?'

'Yeah, back to Wales. In the middle of the night.'

'Are ye serious?' Sorcha was shocked.

''Fraid so.'

'But . . .'

'But what?'

'Oh, nothing.' Sorcha's gaze slipped back to the sea. She picked up a pebble and fired it at the water. Hard. And it didn't bounce, not even once.

'Can I sit by you?' Huw asked her.

'Suppose so,' said Sorks, without enthusiasm. 'Long as it's not contagious.'

'What?'

'The throat.'

'Oh that . . . no.' He shook his head. 'It's not.'

Huw plumped himself down next to her. Careful not to breathe in her direction, in case it scared her off. Sorcha edged away slightly, nevertheless. There was a long silence.

'You OK, Sorks?' he said, sensing her discomfort. 'I can go if you want.'

'No, it's not that . . .' She'd still never really looked at him.

'What is it then?'

'It's just . . .' Sorcha sighed, deeply.

'What?'

'I'm a bit surprised, that's all. I didn't expect Huw to up and leave like that.'

'Yeah, it came as a bit of a shock to me, too.'

'I knew he was heading back soon, but . . .' Scorcha frowned at the horizon like it was asking her some sort of complicated question.

And Huw's mobile went off.

*

'Kath!'

'How are you, babes?'

'I'm fine. How's Nain?'

'She's on the mend. I'll have to stay here a few

more days, I'm afraid, but she'll be fine. Her arm's in plaster, and she's got a hell of a sore head and a load of stitches, but nothing time won't heal, thank God.'

'That's great. Tell her I'm thinking of her.'

They chatted a while longer, before ringing off.

'Bye, Kath. Love you.'

'Love you too, bach.'

*

A silence. Then, 'Who's Kath?'

Oh shoot. Huw'd completely forgotten Sorks was sitting next to him. Forgotten to sound croaky, too.

'Just . . . someone.'

'Someone ye send your love to? I didn't think ye had a girlfriend, Marcus.'

'I don't . . .'

'No need to do a reddener,' said Sorks, seeing him flush. 'I'm just a bit surprised, that's all.'

'Why?' Huw raised his eyebrows. 'Am I too ugly or something?'

'No!' Now it was Sorcha's turn to be embarrassed. 'Course not.'

'You said last night I was too ugly to be Daisy's brother.'

'Oh come on, Marcus. Ye know I was only having ye on. It's just – ye seem a bit shy to have a girlfriend.'

'Do I? Anyway, Kath's not my girlfriend. She's . . . a relative. We're related.'

'What, like a cousin, you mean?'

'Yeah. Something like that.'

He could tell she wasn't convinced.

'Marcus . . .'

'Yeah?'

'There's something about ye . . .'

'How do you mean?'

'Not sure . . .' She frowned. 'I think ye've changed, like . . .'

And Huw realised, at that moment, that there was something about Sorcha, too. Something that made it feel wrong, all wrong, to be spinning her a bunch of lies.

Something that made him want to tell her the truth, the whole truth and nothing but . . .

'Actually, she's my mam,' he said.

'Yer ma?'

'Yeah.'

'But . . .'

'I'm Huw.'

'Ah, stop . . .'

'No, really. I am.'

'Course ye're not. Do ye think I'm an eejit, Marcus?'

Huw said nothing.

She was really staring at him now. 'Are ye serious?'

'I'm serious. I'm Huw.'

'Huw, in Marcus's clothes?'

He nodded.

'Nah!' She shook her head. 'You're having me on.'

'It's true. I can prove it to you.'

'How?'

'I can tell you a secret. In Welsh.'

'Go on then.'

He leant over. 'Ti'n canu fel angel,' he whispered.

'What did ye say?' She moved in closer, to hear him.

'Ti'n canu fel angel, ac rydw i'n leicio bod gyda ti.'

'Sounds nice,' said Sorcha, smiling. 'What does it mean?'

'Oh, I can't tell you that,' said Huw, trying to prevent himself blushing. 'It's a secret, remember?'

'Even from me?'

''Fraid so.'

'Hey, Marcus?'

'Yeah . . . I mean, no . . .'

'Did Huw teach ye to say that?'

'I am Huw, Sorks! How many times do I have to tell you?'

Long silence. 'I suppose it's just possible,' she said at last. 'Ye really are the dead spit of one another, aren't ye?'

'So it seems.'

'So, if ye're Huw . . . And I'm not saying ye are, but . . . Well, I'd never have known, if ye hadn't said.'

'So it seems.'

'But how . . . I mean . . .' She pointed at his clothes. 'Why?'

Huw explained, about the plan, about how it had all gone wrong.

And Sorcha's face went from quizzical to delighted as she listened.

'That's deadly!' she said, when he'd finished.

'Is it?' said Huw, with a frown. 'It was only supposed to be a bit of fun. Till Marcus disappeared.'

'So ye're telling me shy-boy Marcus is in Wales, at your school, pretending to be ye!'

''Fraid so.'

'Well, ye're a couple of fly boys, aren't ye?'

Huw shrugged his shoulders.

'And that leaves ye, stuck here. With me.'

'Suppose so.' Huw made a face. Then smiled.

Another long silence.

'Hey, Huw?'

'Yeah?'

'Know what?'

'What?'

'I think I maybe believe ye.'

'You do?'

'Yeh. And you know what?'

'What?'

'I think I'm maybe glad.'

'You are?'

'Yeh. Glad ye're still here.'

'Why's that?'

'Oh just . . . Ye know . . .'

She leaned her head into his shoulder. And he knew.

*

'Hey, Huw . . .' she asked him. 'Why'd ye run away last night?'

'Huh?'

'When I kissed ye?'

'When you what?'

'I gave ye a little kiss at the sing-song, and ye upped and ran! Don't tell me ye don't remember!'

'I don't, Sorks. It didn't happen.'

'Course it did!' Her eyes flared.

'Listen, Sorks. Read my lips. It . . . wasn't . . . me.'

And then she got it. 'Oh no!' she gasped. 'Ye don't mean to tell me it was Marcus!' Her mouth hung open. And then she collapsed into laughter.

'He's a bit shy,' said Huw, laughing too.

'A bit? He took off like a house on fire! I thought I must have had stinky-cheese breath or something. I can't believe it – I kissed Marcus!'

Long silence.

'So you thought it was me?' Huw asked her.

'Duh. Course I did, stupid.'

'And that would have been all right? Kissing me, I mean?'

Sorcha didn't answer him. Just smiled her little smile.

And Huw smiled, too.

18

Da Iawn, Huw Bach

Aberystwyth, Ceredigion, Wales

'Bore da, Huw!'

'Eh . . . bore da, Mrs Jenkins,' said Marcus. 'How are you this morning?'

'Sut wyt ti?' Gareth's mam went on, ignoring the English of his response.

'Eh . . . iawn, diolch . . .' Marcus managed to reply.

'Da iawn, bach. I told you, you'd be fluent by Monday!' The woman praised him. 'All you needed was a bit of practice. Are you looking forward to school?'

'Eh, yeah . . . sort of . . .'

'It'll be fine. You'll be fine.' She came across the room, noticing his unease. 'I'm sorry I'm not Kath, cariad, but it's the best I can do. Here, give us a cwtsh, you poor dab.'

Marcus wondered why she was calling him a trainer – she hoped it wasn't anything to do with not having been able to work the shower. But the hug was quite nice, really, in a being-hugged-by-the-mother-of-someone-you-don't-even-know sort of a way. Part cosy. Part confusing. It was a while since Marcus had had much of a hug off of his own ma, what with her being so busy and all – it always seemed to be Daisy got the cuddles, if anyone did – so he let himself sink into the warmth of it.

'Thanks. I mean, diolch yn fawr, Mrs Jenkins. Thanks for everything.'

'That's what friends are for. And do call me Ceri. All this Mrs Jenkins business is terribly formal.'

'Kerry as in Ireland?' asked Marcus.

'You're not the first to crack that joke, Huw bach, and you won't be the last.'

What joke? thought Marcus.

In the middle of which, Gareth made his way down for breakfast. 'Oh, he's not on about Ireland again, is he?' he said, overhearing the tail end of the conversation. 'He never shuts up about it, Mam,' he said in Welsh. 'I'd say he'd rather be there than here, and that's the truth of it.'

'All right, Huw?' said Gareth, reverting to English.

Marcus nodded. 'Yeah, I'm fine.'

'All set for school?'

He nodded again.

'Chwarae teg, boys, you both look very smart in your uniforms,' said Ceri, proudly. 'Off you go, then.' She ruffled Gareth's hair. 'Hold your heads high and remember, just because you're new doesn't mean you're stupid. Look out for one another, keep your eyes and ears open, and enjoy it. And I'll see you both at four o'clock.'

She gave Gareth an extra-special hug, then she kissed them both – which was nice of her, thought Marcus, considering she'd only just met him.

And off they went to face the dreaded moment in anyone's life: FIRST DAY AT SECONDARY SCHOOL.

19

Language Lessons

Skerries, County Dublin, Ireland

'Right,' said Daisy, preparing Huw. 'When the teacher's calling out everyone's name, you say, "Anseo".'

'Ann-shuh?'

'That's right. It means here. So I'll be the teacher and you be the pupil.' She pretended to put on a pair of glasses and pick up the register. 'Huw?' she called out, in her best teacherly voice.

'Anseo,' replied Huw, just as he'd been told.

'No! No! No!'

'Why, why, why?' asked Huw. 'Didn't I say it right, miss?'

'Oh, you said it right, all right, but you're not Huw, you eejit – you're Marcus! You won't last five minutes.'

'Yeah, sorry. Let's try it again, then.'

'Right, class,' said Daisy, putting on her firm-but-kind teacherly voice once more. 'I'm just going to check everyone's here. When I call your names, you're to answer, loud and clear. Now, Huw – are you with us today?'

No response.

'Oh,' said Daisy, pretending to be surprised. 'Does anyone know where Huw is?'

Still no response.

'Oh dear, maybe he's ill.' Her voice switched from sympathy to impatience. 'Or off on holiday, again. It's very annoying, all these young people going off on holiday when they're supposed to be in school.' She frowned over the top of her pretend glasses at her pretend class. 'Marcus? Are you here?'

'Anseo, miss,' said Huw, grinning.

'Maith thú, Huw,' said Daisy, becoming Daisy again. 'Very good.' And she burst into a fit of the giggles.

'What's so funny?' asked Huw, frowning.

'Maith thú, Huw!' said Daisy. 'It's like a tongue-twister. You try it.'

'My who, Huw,' said Huw, laughing.

'So what do they say in Wales instead of "anseo",
when the teacher's calling out everyone's names?'
Daisy asked him.

'Yma,' Huw told her.

'Umma,' repeated Daisy. 'Like in Wrigley's?'

'Huh?'

'Chewing gumma.'

Huw laughed. 'So what else'll I need to know
when I get to school?' he asked.

'Hmmm.' Daisy was thinking. 'Let's see now. Can
you count, boy?'

'Of course I can. One . . . two . . . three . . .'

'No.' Daisy giggled. 'I mean in Irish, y'eejit!'

'Hardly,' said Huw. 'But I've a feeling you're going
to try and teach me, miss.'

'I think I'd better,' said Daisy, nodding, as she put
herself back into teacher-mode. 'You won't get far in
life if you can't even count, child.' She glared at him
over her pretend glasses. 'So repeat after me, young
Marcus. A haon, a do, a tri . . .'

'A hayn, a doe, a tree,' repeated Huw. 'That's
OK. I can manage that all right. It's quite like Welsh.'

'Why? What is it in Welsh?' Daisy asked him,
intrigued.

'Un, dau, tri. . .'

'Een, dye, tree . . .' she repeated, forgetting to be a teacher again. 'Hey, you're right, Huw – it's nearly the same! I tell you what, let's count to ten. You say them in Welsh and I'll say them in Irish, and we'll see how close they are.'

'OK,' said Huw. 'Un – that's one . . .'

'It's a haon in Irish,' said Daisy, nodding. 'Sort of the same.'

'Two is dau.'

'A do,' said Daisy, nodding again. 'We're getting closer.'

'Three is tri,' said Huw.

'Are you serious? That's what it is in Irish, too – a trí!' said Daisy, delighted.

'The perfect spit, just like you and Marcus! What's four then?'

'Pedwar.'

'Pedwar?' Daisy shook her head as if he'd said it wrong. 'No, we say a ceathair. And five's a cúig.'

'A kooig?' said Huw. It was his turn to shake his head. 'Ours is pump – spelled pump, pronounced pimp.'

'Pimp!" said Daisy, laughing. 'Funny name for a number! Six is a sé.'

'A shay?' said Huw. 'It's chwech in Welsh.'

Daisy tried to say it, but all she managed was a hissy sound.

Huw laughed. 'What's seven in Irish, then?' he asked her. 'Let's see if they're twinnies, too, like three was.'

'A seacht,' said Daisy.

'We say saith,' Huw told her, nodding. 'Not bad. Eight is wyth.'

'Oyth,' Daisy repeated.

'Da iawn,' said Huw, impressed at her accent. 'Very good.'

'In Irish it's a hocht,' Daisy told him.

'Ah,' said Huw. 'So you've got huchs in your language too! What's nine, then?'

'A naoi.'

'A knee?' He pointed at his knee, and smiled. 'Ours is naw. Not a million miles away.'

'And ten's a deich,' Daisy told him.

'In Welsh it's deg,' said Huw. 'Nearly the same, again. That's one spit and a load of nearlies!'

'Will you remember them?' Daisy asked him.

'Shouldn't think so,' said Huw, shrugging his shoulders. 'It'd probably be easier if they were all completely different from the Welsh. But because some are the same and others are totally different, I'm bound to get in a complete muddle. I think I'll just pretend I'm a bit thick, and can't count.'

'Marcus isn't thick,' said Daisy, sticking up for her big brother. 'Though he can be a bit of a daydreamer, sometimes.'

'OK, I'll do all dreamy, and they'll think I'm Marcus, lost in his own little world.'

20

Eeny Meeny Bore Da

Ysgol Pendinas, Aberystwyth, Ceredigion, Wales

'Gareth Jenkins . . .' said the teacher, reading from his list. All the new kids were sitting in the hall, waiting to be told which registration class to go to. 'Cymraeg.'

'I'm in the Welsh class,' whispered Gareth to Marcus, sitting next to him. 'I wonder which one you're in.'

'Huw Davies . . .' said the teacher, a few names later. 'Cymraeg.'

Marcus was lost in a daydream and didn't even recognize his name – his assumed name, that is. So that it was only Gareth, nudging him in the side and whispering 'You're with me,' that alerted him to catastrophe.

'What, Welsh? No, it can't be!' Marcus jumped to his feet. 'EXCUSE ME, SIR!' he called out.

Everyone turned to stare. This was big school. Scary teachers. You weren't supposed to just jump up and interrupt.

'Excuse me, sir, but I can't possibly be in the Welsh class!' He looked round, despairingly. 'I don't know any Welsh!'

'Who's that shouting?' said the teacher, peering over his glasses, round the room. He'd already called out three more names.

'It's Marc— eh, Huw, sir. Huw Davies.'

'Sit down, boy! Of course you speak Welsh!' He frowned at his list. 'It says here you've spent six years at Ysgol Gynradd, Machynlleth. It says here you're fluent.'

'No. I promise, sir. It must be a mistake, sir. All I can do is count, and I'm not sure I can even do that very well.' He thought he'd better show him. 'Eh . . . Eeny, meeny . . .' There was a giggle. A load of giggles.

'Eeny, meeny, bore, da . . .' he stumbled.

And the whole hall, apart from the two stony-faced teachers up at the front, burst into fits of barely controlled laughter.

'It's the best I can do, I'm afraid, sir,' said Marcus, shrugging his shoulders. 'I'd be lost in the Welsh class, see. I wouldn't have a clue what anybody was on about.'

The teacher looked flustered. There wasn't time for any of this. It was making him look indecisive. New boys and girls were normally so nervous – with so much, so new, happening all around them, and the constant fear of making a fool of themselves – that they did exactly what you told them without batting an eyelid. You could order them to go and climb the Eiffel Tower, jump off, and use their pencil cases as parachutes, and they'd trek out of the room, mild-mannered as sheep, intent on doing their damnedest to carry out your instructions to the very letter.

So what was going on here, then? Why was this annoying child being so awkward? Why wouldn't he just shut up, for goodness sake?

The trouble was, the teacher realised, that he was losing control. And if there's one thing a teacher has to avoid at all costs, especially on the first day of term, with a bunch of brand-new wet-behind-the-ears year sevens, it's losing control. Because if you can't control a bunch of snivelling new ones, you can't control anyone. And as any teacher knows, even one straight out of college, if you lose control of your class even once, you've lost them forever.

He had an urgent whispered conversation with the other teacher standing next to him – the grumpy-looking female one who seemed to disapprove of everyone and everything, him included.

'All right,' he said, eventually, raising his voice to quell the muttering. 'I'll make one exception. But just this one. Everyone else is in the class they're appointed to, and NO ARGUING! Now sit down, boy. And BE QUIET!'

'Phew,' whispered Marcus to Gareth. 'That was a close one.'

'You're off your head, boy!' muttered Gareth, in return.

*

'Huw!'

He'd found his way through the maze of corridors to his classroom. A girl sat herself down on the chair next to him. Marcus looked up at her.

'Why'd you switch out of the Welsh class?' she

asked him, breathlessly. 'Was it really so you could be with me?'

'Eh, yeah, suppose so,' said Marcus. He'd never seen her in his life before, but it seemed the right thing to say.

'Oh, Huw,' said Alice, giving him a lovely cross-eyed smile. He realised she was pretty, in a gawky sort of a way. 'That was really kind of you. I've been so nervous about coming up to Pendinas, especially as you're the only person I know here. And then when I found out we'd be in different classes, I was so upset.'

'Yeah, well . . .'

'You were so brave, facing up to those two horrible teachers – and so funny, making up that story about not even being able to count in Welsh.' She burst out laughing. 'Eeeny, meeny, bore, da . . .' she said, mimicking him. 'You sounded such a dork!'

'Did I?'

'Yeah, it was brilliant! I never knew you were such a good liar!'

'Oh, right,' said Marcus, frowning. 'So how come they didn't try and put you in the Welsh class too, then,' he asked her, 'if they think everyone from

Mach . . .?' (as in lough, as in loch as in Neagh, he reminded himself).

'It's only if you're first-language Welsh,' she told him, 'or if you've been in the area long enough, and your teachers say you're pretty much fluent.'

'So how long have you . . .?'

Alice gave him a funny look. 'What's up, Huw? You haven't seriously lost your memory, have you? It's only a year since I moved up from Essex – you know that! My Welsh is absolutely rubbish!'

'So's mine,' said Marcus.

'Yeah, yeah,' said Alice, nudging him. 'It'll be our little secret, lover boy.'

Lover boy? Marcus blushed to the roots of his toe nails.

Luckily, at that very moment, their new teacher strolled into class, so no one noticed him doing a beamer. They were all way too caught up in first-day-at-new-school terror/excitement to be worried about anyone but themselves.

But unluckily – very unluckily indeed – Marcus recognized the teacher instantly as the grumpy one from the hall. She banged her briefcase down hard on the desk, cast her eyes around the class, and settled her steely gaze on Marcus. And the meaning of the look she gave him was unmistakeable.

'I didn't want you, boy,' it said.

'I wasn't supposed to have you,' it said.

'You're going to regret making my colleague in the hall look a complete and utter fool, and threatening the cool calm efficiency of first-day registration,' it said.

'Oh, yes, I shall see to it, dear little sweet little new boy who thinks he's oh-so-clever, that you regret what you've just done, every day of the rest of your school career,' it said.

And the redness of poor Marcus's features, under the metallic glare of her lifeless eyes, turned to stone-cold white.

21

Finn versus the Bogtrotter

*National School, Skerries,
County Dublin, Ireland*

'Hi, Marcus.'

'Oh, eh . . . hi.' At least Huw didn't make the mistake of not recognizing his new name. 'Howya doing?'

'Great,' said the girl. 'Did you have a good summer?'

'It was cool, yeah.'

'I didn't see you about.'

'No, I was away. Just back from Allihies, actually. Over in West Cork. You know – the other side of the country,' he added, helpfully.

'I do know where Cork is,' said the girl, giving him a funny look. 'How'd it go?'

'Great, really good. You ever been?'

'No. We went to Brittany, again. Staying in a gîte with the cousins.'

'In a what?'

'A gîte. Like a farmhouse. It was lovely. Had its own swimming pool, too.'

'Cool!'

'No, quite warm, actually.' She smiled.

'Massive!' said Huw.

'Are you taking the mick, Marcus?'

'Course not. Why?'

'Well it's hardly massive to you, considering you've a pool in your very own back garden.'

'Oh yeah, whoops!' Marcus must have been exaggerating again. Quick, change the subject, Huw, before you make another dumb mistake. 'So, eh, Brittany! Sounds good. Allihies is nice too, though. We go every year. Stay in the hostel.'

'Hey, Marcus.' The girl smiled, like she was really happy all of a sudden. 'It's nice, chatting together like this, isn't it? Maybe we should do it a bit more.'

'Yeah, maybe.' Oh heck – he'd forgotten what a dork Marcus was with girls.

Then, 'Marcus . . .?' She went all hesitant.

'Mmm?'

'Do you . . . maybe . . .

'What?'

'Well, I was just wondering . . .'

'What?'

'Do you want to go out with me?' she blurted.

'Huh?' Huw couldn't believe his ears.

'Well . . .' The girl was blushing now. 'I was hoping it might be you, asking me maybe, but . . .'

'I suppose I am a bit . . .'

'Shy?' The girl nodded. 'Yeah, but that's OK,' she said, with a smile. 'It's one of the things I like about you, really. So what's changed, Marcus?'

'Changed?'

'Yeah. How come you've been standing here for . . .' she looked at her watch, 'oh, at least three minutes, without doing a runner on me?'

Huw shrugged his shoulders.

Suddenly the girl's face went from embarrassed to angry. 'You've gone and done it, Marcus O'Malley, haven't you?'

'Done what?'

'You've gone and met a girl!'

'A girl?'

'Yeah, someone like me,' she said. 'Only not me. You've gone and met a real live girl, and had a real live conversation with her and everything . . .'

'Everything?'

'Yeah, I can see it in your face – you've gone and got yourself a girlfriend! On holiday, where no one knows you – haven't you? Don't lie to me, Marcus . . .'

Huw didn't know what to say. For one, he wasn't Marcus. But he couldn't tell her that, now could he?

For two, if he did say he'd got himself a girlfriend, maybe at least it'd get this one off his back.

But for three, he wasn't exactly sure if he had or not, anyway. I mean, Sorks . . . What was she?

'What's her name?'

'Huh?'

'The one you met on holiday! Tell me her name.'

'Well . . .' Huw decided he'd better come clean, sort of. It was the only way this girl'd give him a break, by the look of it. 'It's Sorks, actually.'

'Sorks?'

'It's short for Sorch-a.' Damn. He'd said it wrong.

'Sorch-a! Don't you mean Sorcha?'

'Yeah. Sorry. Sorrika.'

'You got off with her and you can't even say her name properly! What's mine?'

'Yours?'

'Yeah, my name, Marcus. What's my name?' Oh heck – she was getting angry now.

'Eh . . .'

'It's Finn! Say it!'

'Finn.' There. Now would she please stop shouting at him.

'Is she pretty?'

'Huh? Oh, yeah . . . I suppose . . .'

'You don't sound too sure. Prettier than me?'

Huw looked at her. 'Different,' he said.

'Different,' repeated Finn, like it wasn't exactly the highest compliment she'd ever been paid. 'Different good or different bad?'

'Well, just different,' mumbled Huw.

'Of course she's different! I hardly thought we'd be identical twins! I mean, you're hardly likely to go all the way to Cork and meet the perfect spit of someone from here, now are you?'

'Well . . .'

'So you and this Sorks – are you going out with her? Like, really going out with her?'

'Eh . . .'

'Is she a good kisser?'

'What?'

'I said, is this girl you met a good kisser?'

'Finn!'

'At least you remember my name. Now, answer me, Marcus O'Malley, because I really want to know. Is this Sorch-a . . .' She pronounced it the wrong way, just to annoy him, 'good at kissing or not?'

'Well, eh. I wouldn't really know.'

'Why, because you didn't kiss her, or because you haven't much to compare it with?'

'Eh . . .' Huw looked at the ground to cover his embarrassment.

And then, taking him completely by surprise, Finn leant forward and pecked him on the lips.

Suddenly they were both blushing furiously, avoiding each other's eyes. Huw didn't know what to say. What to do with himself.

'So you and this Sorks . . .' It was Finn who pulled herself together first. 'Are you going out with her or not?'

'Well, eh . . .'

'You don't sound too sure any more.'

'Em . . .'

'I'd say maybe not, by the sound of it. Because don't forget, I'm here, right beside you . . .'

'Yeah?'

'And she's hundreds of miles away,' said Finn, before a shadow of doubt crept across her face. 'Unless . . .'

'Unless what?'

'Unless . . . she was on holiday, too. Unless she's actually from round here, too?'

'No. She's from Allihies,' Huw reassured her.

'Right. Good. So tell me this, Marcus,' said Finn, looking mightily relieved. 'Are you going to save yourself for this once-a-year bogtrotter, or would you rather go out with me?'

Oh heck, thought Huw. How am I going to get out of this one?

And then, just in time, the bell rang for class.

Phew!

22

Library Cards

Skerries, County Dublin, Ireland

'Hi, Marcus, how was school?'

Huw was buried deep in a book. Not hearing his name, he didn't respond.

'I thought you'd read that one, just the other week,' said Marcus's mum, catching sight of the title.

Whoops. Caught out again. 'Yeah,' said Huw, 'but it was so good I thought I'd read it again.'

*

When he'd finished it – Huw was a speedy reader, and it was only short – he wandered down to the library. He'd seen it on the way to school with Daisy.

It turned out there was a whole load of good stuff on Marcus's shelves, but Huw just had a thing about libraries. He loved sitting there, surrounded by all the books he'd never read, and loads of ones he might. He loved the browsing, the possibilities, the freedom of it. He loved watching what other people chose. Basically he just loved books, more than just about anything else, so that a whole building dedicated to them was his idea of something close to heaven. So that in a time of stress, like now, a library was the calmest, happiest, closest-to-home place he was likely to find.

He spent an age browsing, chose a few interesting-looking ones, and took them to the desk.

The librarian smiled up at him. 'Ticket?'

Huw rummaged around in his pockets. 'Sorry, I seem to have lost it.'

'Never mind. What's your name?' said the woman, which took Huw by surprise. How could she not know Marcus? She must be new here.

'Marcus O'Malley,' said Huw, smiling back at her.

'O'Malley . . . O'Malley . . . Sorry, there's nobody under the name of Marcus O'Malley here,' said the by-now-frowning librarian, scrolling down her computer screen.

'There must be!' said Huw. 'He's lived here for . . . I mean, I've lived here for ages.'

'No, sorry.' The woman shook her head. 'You're definitely not on the list, but I can give you a form to fill in if you want to join. You just need to get your parents to sign at the bottom, and then you can borrow up to four books. I'm afraid I can't let you take these ones till you bring it back, but I'll keep them under the counter for you for a few days. Is that all right?'

'Yeah, sure. Thanks.' Huw turned to go.

'You will come back now, won't you?' said the friendly librarian. 'We don't want to lose a new reader.'

'I'll be back.'

So Huw left a library empty-handed, for probably the first time in his life.

*

'Hey, Daisy, how come Marcus isn't in the library?' he asked her, when he got back to the house.

'What would he be doing in the library?' Daisy hissed. 'Sure, he's in Wales, y'eejit!'

'I know that! I mean, how come he's not a member?'

'Oh, we never use libraries in our family. If there's something we want to read, we just go out and buy it. Or get it on the internet.'

Ah. So that's what it's like being rich, thought Huw.

*

Roddy and Stick came home. They grabbed some food and went out again.

Leah came in with a friend, cooked up a pizza and took it up to her room.

Only Huw and Daisy ate at the table. Even Marcus's mum didn't join them. She was waiting to eat with her husband when he got back from work, late as usual.

Hmm, thought Huw. They don't hang about, this lot, do they? They're rushing and racing all over the place, but nobody stops to talk. Or play. Or just be.

I mean, they don't actually choose to spend much time together.

*

He went up to his room. Played on the computer for about five minutes. Got bored.

Switched on the TV for about three minutes. Got bored. Went downstairs. There was nobody there.

Went back up to his room. Took another book down from the shelf. Started reading.

Phone went diddly dee. A text message from Marcus.

Txt Msgs

Marcus: Wots wiv u n alice?

Huw: Alice b? Nufin y?

M: She cald me lovrboy

H:

M: R u goin out wiv her?

H: No way

M: She fancies u

H: U mor like

M: Dont u mind?

H: Go 4 it yejit. So wots wiv u n Finn then?

M: Finn?

H: She sure as hell fancies u

M: No way. She's nice, tho

H: She does. Weird

M: Wots weird?

H: Both of us getting off wiv girls, sort of. De wrong girls

M: Yeh i C wot U mean

H: Wot apens me apens u

M: Wot apens u, apens me 2. We're the perfect spit

H: Hows skul?

M: Big n welsh n scary

H: U in cymraeg?

M: No way. Hows urs?

H: Easy peasy kidz stuf

M: U O me €€€

H: Y? R u still undr covr?

M: Yeh

H: Me 2 cept Daisy. So u o me £££

M: No way. Daisy counts. Hows yr gran?

H: OK I think

M: Whens yr ma home?

H: Dunno

M: Call it quits when shes bk?

H: U had enuf?

M: Sort of. Its fun, but messy

H: OK lets get it sorted, b4 we r in 2 deep.

23

Coming Clean

Skerries, County Dublin, Ireland

'Hey, Finn.'

They were at the school gates. It was time for Huw to come clean.

'Marcus! How's it going?'

'OK. I've something to tell you.' Huw was looking sheepish.

'Yeah?'

'You won't like it.'

'I won't?' Finn's eyes lost some of their sparkle.

'Well . . .'

'Get on with it, Marcus. You don't want to go out with me. That's what you're trying to say, isn't it?'

'Eh . . .'

'You're saving yourself for that bogtrotter of yours? The one who's a better kisser than me?'

Huw looked at his feet. 'Well, eh . . . her or Alice.'

'Alice! You mean there's two of them?'

'Only sort of . . .'

'Sort of! Look, either there is or there isn't. But what's going on round here, Marcus? A few weeks ago you couldn't even look at a girl – now you're juggling three of us!'

'No, listen . . . I know you'll find this hard to believe, Finn, but it's actually a whole lot more complicated than that, even.'

'More complicated than THAT?' Finn's eyebrows were sky-high by now.

'Yeah, you see . . .' Huw wasn't sure how to go about telling her. 'I'm not really what you think I am.'

There was a long pause. A very long pause.

'Oh, Marcus,' said Finn, gently. 'You're not . . .'

'What?'

'Well, you know . . . I mean, it's all right, of course, but . . .'

Huw suddenly understood what she was getting at. 'No!' he said, flushing. 'Of course I'm not!'

'You are, aren't you?' said Finn. 'That's what all this is about.'

'It's not, I'm not!' Huw insisted. 'No, what I meant to say just now wasn't that I'm not really WHAT you think I am – more that I'm not really WHO you think I am.'

Finn heard him. But surely she hadn't heard him right. 'You're not Marcus O'Malley?'

'Exactly! You've got it!' Huw was nodding like a demented bulldog in the back of a 4 by 4. 'I'm someone else, see! Someone who only LOOKS like Marcus O'Malley!'

Finn sighed. 'Give me a break, Marcus. I mean, if you want to dump me, just dump me – not that we ever actually got around to going out together anyway . . .'

'No really, Finn, I'm telling you the truth. I'm the perfect spit of him – everyone says so. We're just about identical. Even our mothers can hardly tell us apart.'

'Oh, Marcus.' Finn looked at the ground. 'I always knew it'd be hard getting you to open up, but I never thought that when you did, you'd turn out to be such a liar.'

'No, really. Listen to me, Finn,' Huw pleaded. 'I'M NOT MARCUS!'

'Tell me you don't want to go out with me,' she said, refusing to listen to him. 'Tell me Sorcha – or this Alice, whoever she is . . . Oh, Marcus – just tell me the truth!'

'I'm not lying, Finn.' Huw dug his hand deep into his pocket. 'I can prove it to you.'

Pulling out his wallet, he drew out a photo of himself and handed it to her.

Finn examined it closely, for a long time. 'Who's this with you?' she asked.

'My mam,' said Huw. 'It's me and my mam.'

'That's not your ma, Marcus. I've met your ma. And you don't call her your mam, either. You've never called her mam.'

'That's because I'm not Marcus! And I usually call her Kath, anyway, but that's another matter. We're outside our house. In Machynlleth.'

'You're where?'

'Machynlleth. It's in Wales. Here, look . . .' He drew out his library card. 'Huw Davies,' it said. '1 Penrallt Street, Machynlleth.' And it had a photo on it – a photo of him.

'H . . .' Finn tried to read the name.

'Huw,' he told her.

'That's not how you spell Huw.'

'It is, in Wales.'

'Huw Davies,' read Finn, looking from him to the photo, from the photo to him. 'Are you serious? This is you?'

Huw nodded. 'It's what I've been trying to tell you, all this time.'

'And you're not Marcus O'Malley?'

'Definitely not Marcus O'Malley.'

'This is weird!' Finn turned the library card over and over in her hand. 'So what's all this writing on the back?' she asked him. 'I can't read a word of it.'

'That's 'cos it's in Welsh,' said Huw. 'It's a different language.'

'Yeah, I've heard of Welsh. But can you actually speak it?'

'Course I can. I've lived there all my life. Here, I'll read it to you . . .'

*

'That's really weird,' said Finn, when he'd finished. 'Doesn't sound like any language I've ever heard.'

'That's Welsh for you.'

'And if it's true . . . If you're not just Marcus, having me on – if you're somebody who looks exactly like him, and is somehow here, instead of him – then this whole thing is really REALLY weird.'

Huw shrugged.

'So you're this Huw character? You expect me to believe that?'

'Huw Davies ydw i,' he replied in Welsh. 'That's me.'

'So how come you're here, Huw Davies?' she said, trying out the name to see if it fitted him. 'Not in this place – Mach . . .'

Finn was struggling, as you very well might be, when your world's turned upside down and back to front. And on top of all that you're trying to pronounce the word Mach . . . Mach . . .

'Machynlleth,' said Huw, helpfully. 'I was over on holiday in County Cork, me and Kath.'

'Your ma?'

'Yeah, my mam. So we got as far as Allihies, where I met up with the famous Marcus O'Malley.'

'The perfect spit, you say?'

'Identikit,' said Huw, nodding. 'But we didn't realise. Not till Daisy pointed it out.'

'Marcus's little sister?'

'Yeah. You know her?'

Finn nodded.

'Everyone kept saying they couldn't tell us apart,' Huw continued. 'So, after a while, Marcus and me hatched this crazy plan to do a swap. Just for a few hours, like. Just for a laugh.'

'A swap?'

'Yeah. Me pretend to be him. Him pretend to be me. See what it's like, living in someone else's shoes. Me in a big Irish family with lots of dosh . . .'

'Yeah, they're loaded, those O'Malleys, aren't they?'

'Sure are – compared to me and Kath, anyway. So the plan was I'd kip in the hostel, with his two brothers.'

'Roddy and Stick? They're gross! You wouldn't get me within a million miles of either of them. Especially in the dark.'

'Too right,' said Huw. 'So, as I say, I'd be a part of Marcus's family, just for the night – or as long as it took to be found out, anyway. And Marcus'd just be with Kath – my mam, remember – staying in the camper van.'

'You've got a camper? A VW?'

'Yeah.'

'That's cool. Cool idea, too, doing a swap.' Finn was impressed, at last. 'So how'd you get Marcus to agree?'

'Agree! It was his idea in the first place.'

'It was? I'd have thought Marcus was way too scaredy-ba to come up with a plan like that, never mind go through with it.'

'Maybe you don't know him as well as you think you do,' suggested Huw.

'Hmm . . . Maybe he's different on holiday. I'll have to think about heading down to Allihies myself, one of these summers. But what about you, Huw? Weren't you scared?'

'Not scared, no. It was supposed to be just a bit of holiday fun. The trouble is it went too well, really. We both went to bed . . .'

'Wrong beds?'

'Yeah, sort of,' Huw nodded. 'Then Kath got a call in the middle of the night – really urgent, like.

She'd no choice but to head off home to Wales, straight away.'

'Only . . .'

'You guessed it. There was Marcus, sound asleep in the back of the van, pretending to be me. Leaving me, stuck here in Ireland, pretending to be him.'

'And this call?' Finn had her sympathetic look on again.

'It was to tell her my nain's ill.'

'Who's that? Your sister?'

'No, there's only me – well, me and Kath. No, it was my granny. She'd fallen off her bike. Smashed her head on the pavement. She's in hospital.'

'Oh, Marcus – I mean, Huw. You must be so worried.'

'I have been, yeah. But I rang Kath last night. My nain's coming out in a couple of days, and she's agreed to come and stay with us for a while. Till she's better, anyway.'

'Did you tell your ma you're in Ireland?'

'No, I didn't want to worry her. But I'll tell her tonight. It's time this thing was sorted.'

'Yeah.' Finn nodded. 'She needs to know where you are.'

'It all got a bit out of hand,' said Huw. 'But soon I'll be back in Wales, Marcus'll be home here, and it'll be like none of this ever happened.'

'No more wanting to be part of a big Irish family?'

'No way.' Huw shook his head. 'Been there, done that. Didn't think too much of it, as a matter of fact.'

'No place like home, then?'

'That kind of thing,' said Huw. 'Holidays are OK, but it'll be good to get back.'

'So what about this Sorcha you keep going on about? You'll miss her, by the sound of it.'

'Oh, she's just someone else I met in Allihies.'

'Holiday romance?'

'Not really.' Huw felt a blush coming on.

'Hey!' Finn laughed. 'You look even more like Marcus when you do that!'

'Huh?'

'When you do a reddener.'

'Oh, right,' said Huw. 'But anyway, like I was saying . . .'

'. . . you're unavailable,' Finn finished the sentence for him, 'to anyone else.'

Huw nodded. 'Sort of.'

'Except maybe Alice?'

'Oh, she's just someone at school. Back in Wales. Marcus says she likes me.'

'Marcus does?'

'Yeah, he's been texting me. He's taken up my place at my new school.'

'And this Alice . . .?'

'We were at junior school together. She's been getting all friendly with him. But it's not as though she knows it's Marcus. It's just a case of, you know, mistaken identity.'

'So she's a bit like me?'

'How do you mean?'

'Like me, pushing myself onto you, thinking you're Marcus.' She made a face.

'So what's all this about you and Marcus, anyway?' Huw asked her.

'Oh . . .' Finn thought she might as well come clean, seeing as Huw had. 'I've really liked him ever since I moved here. Only he never seems to even notice me.'

'He likes you too, you know.'

'What makes you say that?'

'He said so. When we were texting.'

'How come he even mentioned me?'

'I said I'd met you.'

'And he said he liked me?'

'Sure did.'

'Hmm.' Finn sounded unconvinced. 'How's he getting on, anyway?'

'OK, so far as I can see. No one's even rumbled him yet.'

'They still think he's you?'

'Must do.'

'That's amazing!'

'Yeah. But then, you know how quiet Marcus is,' said Huw. 'Probably just fading into the background, like so much wallpaper.'

'Keeping his head buried deep in a book,' added Finn. 'So did you go out with her, this Sorcha?'

'No.' Huw sighed.

'Sounds like you wish you had.'

'Yeah, maybe. But it's too late now. She'll soon forget she ever met me, if she hasn't already.'

'I don't think so, somehow,' said Finn.

'How come?'

'Just a feeling,' said Finn, with a little smile. 'You could write to her, maybe.'

'Where to? I don't even know her address.'

'Allihies is only a small town, by the sound of it. What's her surname?'

'McNulty.'

'Write to Sorcha McNulty, Allihies, County Cork. That'll get to her.'

'Yeah, but I don't know her post code.'

'Post code? Are you looking for excuses, or what?'

'Course I'm not.'

'Are you afraid she'll say no? That she doesn't want anything more to do with you?'

'No . . . Well, yeah . . . Maybe . . .'

'You might as well know.'

'I suppose.'

'Or you could look her address up in the phone book,' suggested Finn. 'There can't be too many McNultys, even in the back of beyond.'

'Or write to her care of the hostel, I suppose,' said Huw, perking up. 'Seamus knows her. He'd pass it on.'

'Go for it, Huw,' said Finn. 'I like happy endings.'

'OK.' Huw smiled. 'But only if you agree to text Marcus. Right here, right now. Do you want his number?'

Txt Mgs 2

Finn: It's me Finn

Marcus: Finn??

F: Got yer number off Huw. How r u?

M: OK

F: U comin home soon? I miss u

M: U do?

F: 4 sure Huws nice but ur nicer

M: He is? I am?

F: Can I ask u sumfin, Marcus?

M: Yeh

F: Do u like me? Huw sed u sed u did

M: He did?

F: Yeh. So do u?

M: Yeh

F: ! ! ! So do u wanna go out wiv me?

M: R u serious?

F: Course. So do u or dont u?

M: ! ! !

F: Does that mean yeh?

M: Sure does

F: On 1 condition

M: ? ?

F: U talk 2 me! 1st of all on de fon. Then in real life. Even when sum1 else is around. Not always blush n run away. Do u think u can do that?

M: I'll try

F: Not gud enuf. WILL u do it? Really truly

M: OK

F: U promise?

M: X my heart n hope 2 die

F: No worries. Hey, Marcus?

M: Yeh?

F: XXXXXXX

M: !!! Hey, Finn?

F: ? ? ?

M: XX

F: !!! Blush blush! Red as a carrot!

Txt Mgs 3: Sometime Later

Marcus: Hey

Huw: Hey

M: U home?

H: I'm home!!! U2?

M: Gr8st rock&roll band in de universe. Irish, 2!!

H: Ha ha

M: Yeh, I'm home. How's the form?

H: Da iawn.

M: Ur gran?

H: She's fine

M: Kath?

H: Cross at 1st. OK now

M: Skul?

H: Gud. Their surprised my Welsh improved so quick!

M: How's Alice?

H: Just friends

M: & Sorks?

H: In touch

M: Looking gud?

H: Looking gud!

M: C u in Allihies nxt summer?

H: U bet

M: Hey, Huw?

H: What?

M: Me n Finn!!

H: U n Finn??!!

M: De real deal

H: XX??

M: Spit spit!!!

H: Perfect!!!!

About the Author

Malachy Doyle was born in Ireland, but after eighteen years he did his first swap, moving to England to study, pack polo mints, work in advertising and have babies.

At the age of thirty he swapped England for Wales, living in Ciliau Aeron and growing pigs and potatoes. After eight years there, he swapped Ceredigion for Powys, and moved to Machynlleth to be a teacher. After another eight years he swapped counties again, this time to Gwynedd, to live in Aberdyfi and write books.

Eight years later, in the middle of writing *Swap*, he did the Big Swap, returning home to Ireland. He now lives on a tiny island off the coast of Donegal, with his wife Liz and a jet-black cat called Milo.

www.malachydoyle.co.uk